Purchased with

donated funds.

CARL DEUKER

SWAGGER

HOUGHTON MIFFLIN HARCOURT

BOSTON   NEW YORK

The text of this book is set in Minion Pro.

Library of Congress Cataloging-in-Publication Data
Deuker, Carl.
Swagger / Carl Deuker.
p. cm.
Summary: High school senior point guard Jonas Dolan is on the fast track to a
basketball career until an unthinkable choice puts his future on the line.
ISBN 978-0-547-97459-0
[1. Basketball—Fiction. 2. Sexual abuse—Fiction.] I. Title.
PZ7.D493Sw 2013
[Fic]—dc23
2012045062

Manufactured in the United States of America
DOC 10 9 8 7 6 5 4 3 2 1
4500437814

For my mother,
Marie Milligan Deuker,
1923–2007

I would like to thank Ann Rider, the editor of this book, for her advice and encouragement.

PART ONE

1

ALL THIS STARTED ABOUT A year and a half ago. Back then I was a junior at Redwood High in Redwood City, a suburb twenty-five miles south of San Francisco. In those days, before Hartwell, before Levi, I took things as they came, without thinking a whole lot about them. Maybe that's because most of the things that came my way were good.

Take school. I didn't much like my classes at Redwood High, but I did like being the starting point guard on the varsity basketball team. And I loved seeing my name, Jonas Dolan, in print in the sports section of the *Redwood City Tribune*.

The main reason school never seemed to matter too much had to do with my father's job. He made good money working for a sand and gravel company down at the Redwood City harbor. I liked visiting him at work — liked the noise of the cement mixers, the shouts of the men, the nonstop activity of the plant. I figured that once I graduated from high school, my dad would get me a job there. He thought so too; lots of times we talked about working together.

Not that I was a total slacker in the classroom. You can't play if you don't earn your credits, so I studied enough to stay eligible.

Halfway into my sophomore season, I'd cracked the starting lineup on the varsity basketball team. For the rest of that season, I averaged eight points and three assists per game. During the first half of my junior year, I'd pushed those numbers up to eleven and six, making me one of the top four point guards in a decent league.

Then I had my breakout game.

It came in mid-January against Carlmont, a middle-of-the-pack team like us. Everyone expected the game to be a nail-biter, with one team winning by a few points. Instead, we trounced them. I scored fourteen points, pulled down five rebounds, and had nine assists, while turning the ball over only once. It was the best game of my life, but I didn't feel as if I was playing out of my mind. Instead, it was like everybody else on the court was wearing lead shoes, while I was lighter than air.

2

THAT CARLMONT GAME HAD BEEN on a Wednesday night. I floated through school the next day and through practice after school. As I was leaving the gym, I heard Coach Russell's voice. "Jonas Dolan, come to my office."

He sat me down across from him, pulled on his big ears a couple of times, scratched his gray hair, and finally asked me what I planned to do when I finished high school.

"My dad works at the sand and gravel. He can get me a job there."

"No plans for college?"

I didn't like the way Coach Russell said that, as if there was something wrong with people who didn't go to college. "Neither of my parents went to college, and they've done okay."

Coach Russell started waving his hands around, his face reddening. "Completely true, Jonas. I know your dad; I know Robert. He's a hard-working man. And I've met your mom, though I can't say I know her. There's nothing wrong with working with your hands. But you've got your whole life to work. If you go to college, you can be a kid for a while longer. That sand and gravel plant isn't going anywhere."

As he spoke, I thought about what it would be like to work eight hours every single day. Was I ready to do that? Still, I shook my head when he finished. "I'm lucky to get Cs, Coach. I'm no student."

"But you could be a good student, Jonas. I talked to your teachers; they all say that."

After he said this we both sat, the seconds ticking away. Then he leaned forward, a glint in his eyes. "If you could play basketball in college, would that make a difference?"

I was so startled by the thought that I laughed. "Sure it would, but there's no college that wants a six-foot white guy who can't dunk. The worst player on a crappy team like Oregon State is way better than I am."

Coach Russell put his big hands flat on his desk and leaned back. "Jonas, Oregon State is a Division One school. I'm not saying you're D-One material. However, there are three hundred Division Two schools that have basketball teams. Many are top-notch private colleges — great places to get an education. You're a hard-nosed ballplayer; you're the most coachable kid I've had in years; your game is coming on like gangbusters. Those are all qualities that D-Two coaches look for."

As he spoke, a strange thrill raced through me. I was a step slower than the black guys from Oakland and San Francisco I'd played against, but Coach Russell was right — those guys were headed to major colleges. Some of them might even end up in the NBA. They wouldn't even consider Division II ball.

Then reality hit: college costs big bucks.

"Coach, my parents don't have money for something like that."

He smiled. "Ever heard of a scholarship, Jonas? And I mean a full ride — room and board. If you're not interested, then that's that. But if you are, I'll help. Division Two coaches don't come looking for players. I'll need to get some game film of you and write you a letter of recommendation. You'll need to request a copy of your official transcript. If we send all that out to fifty schools, you might get a call or two." He looked at me from under his bushy eyebrows. "You'll never know unless you try."

3

I KNEW MY MOM WOULD BE crazy happy when she heard what Coach Russell had said about the possibility of college, but with my father things were more complicated.

In September, just as school was starting, the chute on my dad's cement mixer had swung free and smacked into his leg. The impact fractured his kneecap and caused internal bleeding in his leg. My dad needed two operations, and afterward his leg had become so infected that the doctors nearly had to amputate. He didn't lose the leg, but when he came out of the hospital, he walked with a limp.

My dad didn't go back to work until November. For a week, he tried to drive a mixer, but he couldn't do it, so his boss gave him an office job as a dispatcher.

I figured everything was okay, but right after the New Year, he started coming home after my mom and I had already eaten, looking both tired and worried. He smiled when he saw me, but it was a forced smile. As soon as I went into the den to watch television, he and my mom would whisper together in the living room, their voices low.

I tried to tune them out, but I couldn't. Was he sick? Not just injured, but really sick? Or was it something else? I'd had friends on the basketball team — Mark Westwood was one of them — whose parents had gotten divorced, and their kids had had no clue it was coming. Was that it?

One night I was watching the Warriors play the Thunder when the front door opened. My dad said hello like he usually did; then he went into the living room, and there was whispering between Mom and him. I tried to concentrate on the game, but my stomach churned with worry. I was about to head to my room to get away when his voice called out. "Come out here, Jonas. You need to know this."

I sat in the big chair across from him; my mom sat next to him on the sofa, her hand in his. He looked at her and then turned to me. "Jonas, two men from the national headquarters of the sand and gravel have been around the past few months. They're both college guys, brainy types whose job is to figure out how to make more money for the company. One idea they're kicking around is to computerize the dispatch part of the business. If they go that route, I could be out of a job."

I looked at him in disbelief. "That's crazy. You've been there twenty-five years. You know more about that place than — "

He raised his hand, signaling me to stop. "Jonas, I'm telling you this because you're not a kid anymore, and you need to know the truth. It's about money, nothing else. But whatever happens, we're going to be fine." He looked at my mom. "We're going to be just fine."

4

THAT CONVERSATION HAD TAKEN PLACE two weeks before the Carlmont game. Ever since then, I'd heard my dad complain to my mom about some change the college guys were proposing. I could hear bitterness in his voice. Now I had to suck up the courage to tell him that I wanted to be a college guy.

I would have done it, too. But as I stepped inside the front door that night, my dad was slumped on the sofa, his face looking more lined than ever. My mom sat in the chair across from him. Her mouth was turned down and her short blond hair was mussed — she works as a hairdresser, so it's never that way. They'd been talking in low voices when I opened the door, but the room fell silent once they saw me.

I said hello, pretending not to have noticed anything, and then headed into the kitchen. My mom followed me, asking me what I wanted to eat. After she'd stuck an enchilada dinner into the microwave, she put silverware on the table in front of me. As she moved around the kitchen, her eyes were watery, as if she was on the verge of tears. That wasn't like her, either. In my whole life, I'd seen her cry only a couple of times.

For the five minutes the frozen dinner spun around on a glass plate, she asked the usual questions about my day. As we talked, I heard my dad in the front room rustling the pages of the newspaper.

When my dinner was ready, my mom sat down across from me. I took a couple of bites before putting down my fork. "Did they fire him?"

She shook her head. "No, they didn't."

"So what's wrong?"

She spoke in a low voice. "They hired a whiz kid from Cal Berkeley. He's going to try to merge customer information and area maps and cement-mixer capacities and traffic flow and who knows what else into some computer software program that would make everything more efficient. If he succeeds, they won't need your dad to figure out the timing or the routes or —" She stopped and shook her head.

5

MY NEXT GAME WAS FRIDAY night against Sequoia High, our cross-town rival. As we came out of the locker room to loosen up, Coach Russell pointed to the top row of the stands. I followed his finger and spotted a stocky man with a movie camera mounted on a tripod. "That's my brother Jim. He'll be filming you."

The place was rocking, lights and sounds filling every inch of the gym, but as I moved through our pregame drills, all I felt was the camera trained on me like a rifle. I looked down at my hands just before tip-off, and they were shaking.

The jitters stayed with me through the opening minutes of the game. On an early fast break, I dribbled the ball off my foot and out-of-bounds. The next possession, I hoisted up an air ball from about twenty-eight feet. "Settle down, Dolan," Coach Russell hollered, palms facing down.

Sequoia's guard, Alex Fuentes, brought the ball up. Just as I went for a steal, Fuentes crossed over on me and drove to the hoop for a lay-up. As he ran back to play defense, Fuentes smirked at me, as if I were nothing.

That smirk snapped me out of my funk. For the rest of the half,

I was in his face on defense and eating him alive on offense. I hit a step-back jumper at the three-minute mark, and then faked the same shot only to blow by him for a lay-up the next time down. We were trailing by seven when Fuentes gave me his little grin again; at halftime we were up by four points. During that stretch, I totally forgot the camera.

And I didn't think about it during the second half, either. A point guard isn't a scorer; my main responsibility was to get the other guys going, particularly Mark Westwood, our center. Early in the third quarter, I gave a couple of nice lobs over the top that resulted in easy dunks. After that, I spread the ball around, getting different guys on the team touches. Everything clicked, and we ended up winning, 58–39. My line: thirteen points, nine assists, and three rebounds.

Afterward Coach Russell high-fived us all. "Great game! Great game!" As the locker room emptied, he motioned for me to stay behind. Once we were alone, he told me he was going to make DVD copies of the video his brother had shot and get them in the mail. "Shouldn't someone edit it first?" I asked. "I screwed up royally in the first quarter."

Coach Russell shook his head. "Trust me, Jonas. Sending a complete game is the way to go. Coaches will know we're not hiding anything. Honesty matters."

That was like Coach Russell, always completely straightforward. I didn't think much of it in those days. I thought all adults were that way. I didn't know then what I know now.

In the locker room, I changed into street clothes and then went to an arcade with Mark where we played video games and talked hoops. "You might make all-league next year," Mark said. "You're playing lights out."

When I returned home later that night, the house was dead quiet. I assumed my parents were asleep, but when I turned on the light, I saw my dad sitting on the sofa with his leg up on an ottoman, a heating pad wrapped around it. The instant the light went on, he took his leg down and unwrapped it.

"You okay?" I said.

"I've been better," he answered. Then he smiled. "I was at your game tonight."

"You were? I didn't see you."

"I had to leave at the end of the third quarter. Damn leg. You stunk it up early, but you sure came on. Did you finish strong?"

"We killed them."

"I figured as much."

In the dark room, in the quiet, I almost told him about the video and the letter to the colleges. But before I could find the words to start, my dad stood. "Well, I'm off to bed. You made your old man proud today, Jonas."

6

I SPENT SATURDAY AT THE YMCA on Hudson Avenue playing pickup games. One odd thing happened: Alex Fuentes, the guard for Sequoia High, came in after I'd been there for half an hour. It was tense between us for a few minutes, but then we both relaxed, and he turned out to be a good guy. "You thought I was dissing you?" he said at the water fountain between games. "I'd never do anything to get anybody ticked off, especially not you. You're the toughest matchup I've had all year."

Monday morning, right before lunch, I got a note calling me to the coaches' office. When I stepped inside, Coach Russell held up a couple of pages of paper and waved them around. "I printed a list of Division Two colleges that give scholarships. There are some in every part of the country. You have any preference as to where you want to go?"

"Wherever you say, Coach."

He shook his head. "No, Jonas, not wherever I say. You're the one who's going to live there."

In fifth grade, I'd done my state report on Vermont, filling twenty pages with pictures of rolling mountains that seemed to be on fire because of the autumn colors of the trees. "Are any in Vermont?" I asked.

"There are a couple in Vermont, and even more in Massachusetts and New Hampshire and Connecticut. But are you sure you want to live in New England? It gets cold there."

I'd never once thought of living in New England, but as soon as he said the words, I somehow knew that New England was the place for me.

"New England," I said.

"New England it is. I'll make fifty copies of this DVD and your transcript, and write a letter of recommendation for you. You'll need to sign up for the SAT. I'll contact the NCAA Clearinghouse and help you get that paperwork done. You can address the manila envelopes in my office during lunch. That I'm not doing for you."

I addressed half the envelopes during lunch and the other half after practice the following day. Then, for the next four games, I played the best basketball I'd ever played in my life.

7

KNEW THAT AT SOME POINT I'd have to tell my mom and dad about Coach Russell's DVD and the letters he'd sent out for me, but I kept putting it off. I waited partly because I'd look like a fool if no coach called, but mainly because my dad was so worried about losing his job. I'd hear him complain to my mom about the guy from Cal Berkeley. "I swear to God, Mary, he looks at me as if I were a piece of broken furniture. If he could, he'd put me out with the trash."

February was rolling by. Before every practice I'd give Coach Russell a look, but he'd only shake his head. When we were alone, he'd tell me to be patient, but the better I played, the more I ached to hear from some school. There was nothing — no interest. The game on the DVD was good; the letter from Coach Russell was good. My lousy grades were the problem; I knew it, and so did Coach Russell. Why had I been such a lazy dog?

Then, on the Friday before Presidents' Day weekend, the door opened during my English class, and I was handed a note telling me to report immediately to the library. Coach Russell was waiting for me by the circulation desk. "Monitor College," he said, his voice excited. "Ever heard of it?"

I shook my head.

"Neither have I. It's in New Hampshire, which is right next to Vermont. Their coach wants to talk to you. Skype."

"When?"

His face broke into a broad smile. "Right now. Mrs. Johnson, the librarian, is setting up a computer." Coach Russell put his big hands on my shoulders and looked me in the eye. "Just be yourself, Jonas."

Monitor's coach was Greg Richter, a young black guy with a close-cropped beard and intense eyes. His basketball questions were easy to answer, but I felt like a fish flopping around in the bottom of a boat once he switched to academics. *How were my reading skills? My math skills? Why had I only taken one lab science class? Could I improve my grades?* Drops of sweat formed on my forehead; my ears rang. Finally I leveled with him. "I've never tried hard, Mr. Richter. But starting right now, I will. I promise."

Silence.

From three thousand miles away, he looked at me as if he were trying to look into my heart. Finally he spoke. "Thanks very much for your time, Jonas. I'd also like to talk to your parents. How about if I call them on Sunday morning? Say ten o'clock your time?"

I gave him my home number, remembered to thank him, and then the computer screen went blue. I turned to Coach Russell, who had been watching from off to the side.

"You did fine," he said.

"You think I've got a chance, even with my grades?"

"He wouldn't have called if your grades were a deal-breaker. Believe me, college coaches are way too busy to waste time."

When I returned home that night, my mom was in the kitchen getting my dinner ready. I couldn't stall any longer, so as she put together a plate of food for me, I told her about Coach Richter and Monitor College.

I kept my voice low, and I said that most likely nothing would come of it, but as I was speaking, she stopped mashing the potatoes and stared at me, her eyes wide. When I finished, she hugged me and then stepped back, taking my hands in hers. "That's wonderful, Jonas. Have you told your father?"

I shook my head. "I'm afraid to."

She tilted her head, puzzled. "Why?"

I shrugged. "You know. The way Dad talks about the college guys from the corporate office. The way the guy from Cal Berkeley is treating him. He hates them. You know he does."

My mom frowned. "Jonas, this is *you*. Nothing could make your dad happier than good things happening to you. Tell him right now."

So I did, and he jumped up and pounded me on the back. "You want to hear something strange," he said. "As I was watching your last game, I thought: *He could play college ball.* I actually considered calling Coach Russell and asking him to get a recruiter out to look at you." My mom came out then, and she hugged me again. Seeing both of them smile made me glad I'd told them. They hadn't smiled like this in a long time.

Eventually, my dad went back to his newspaper and my mom returned to the kitchen. I walked down the hallway to my room, opened my laptop, and logged on to Monitor College's website.

The campus was perched high on a hilltop. All the buildings had ivy crawling up their walls. There were photos of students studying in the library, playing Frisbee on the lawn, and drinking coffee in an espresso shop. I could almost imagine myself walking on those tree-lined paths, my backpack crammed with books.

8

THE SUNDAY PHONE CALL FROM Coach Richter came at the exact minute he said it would. From the kitchen, I heard my dad say that I was dedicated to basketball, honest, and not a hardhead. Next Mr. Richter talked to my mom. The roles changed then; she asked the questions. She must have liked his answers because her head kept nodding up and down.

Finally my dad called me to the telephone. So much was whirling around inside me that I had trouble following Coach Richter's sentences. Still, I did hear the last thing loud and clear. "You'll be getting a detailed letter from me, so keep an eye on the mail."

I hung up, talked to my parents for a while, and then returned to my room. I took out my history book and tried to study, but I couldn't concentrate.

When I'd been younger, working at the sand and gravel had seemed exciting. Driving a mixer, sending cement tumbling down a long chute, filling some big hole — what could be better to a ten-year-old? I wasn't ten anymore, though. Coach Russell had opened my eyes. Work like that would be great for a year or two. But for a lifetime? I thought about my father, about what the work had done to his body, and about how they were treating him now. What would he do if they fired him? He knew cement mixers, but that was all he knew. I didn't know if I'd like college, but that didn't really matter. Richter was giving me a chance to change my life. I couldn't pass up an opportunity like that.

We had a district playoff game, a win-or-go-home game, on Wednesday night against St. Francis in their gym down in Mountain View. The Lancers had lost only twice all year, so we were slated to be the team going home.

The advantage of being an underdog is that nobody expects anything from you. I figured if I played my game — which was scoring a little and passing a lot — we could hang close through three quarters. If you hang close, anything can happen in the fourth quarter. It would be terrific to tell Coach Richter that I'd led my team to a huge upset.

What I didn't anticipate was the intensity of the Lancers' defense. From the opening tip, St. Francis double-teamed me as soon as I crossed midcourt. I'd pass out of the trap, setting up a four-on-three for the other guys. We should have scored in bunches, but my teammates couldn't hit anything. Once guys miss a few open shots, they start thinking, and then they miss everything.

With my teammates struggling, I tried to take over the game. I dribbled too much; I forced up wild shots. Coach Russell called a time-out to settle us, then another one. From ten rows up, I heard my dad yell at me to calm down, but I couldn't. When the horn sounded, ending the first half, we were down, 32–13.

We played better in the second half, but we never cut the lead to fewer than twelve. The final score was 64–46, ending our season with a thud.

On the drive home, my dad told me that my future was bright. I nodded, but an hour later I lay awake reliving all the dumb plays I'd made. If Coach Richter had seen that game, he'd have never called.

9

A WEEK AFTER THE ST. FRANCIS loss, I shot around for a while after school with Mark, and then I walked home. As usual, I checked the mailbox before stepping inside. This time, instead of coming up empty, I pulled out a thick envelope with Monitor College's address in the upper left-hand corner.

Both my parents were at work, so I had the house to myself. I carried the envelope to the kitchen table and carefully opened it. Inside was a letter and a color brochure. I put off reading Richter's letter and first flipped through the brochure. The photographs were similar to the ones I'd seen on their website: ivy creeping up the side of old brick buildings, golden trees lining gravel pathways, pure white snow blanketing a winter landscape. I closed the brochure, took a deep breath, and then read the letter from Coach Richter.

The first paragraph was about basketball. He wrote that his offense required a smart point guard to run a fast-break offense, and that he liked what he saw of me on the DVD, both on offense and defense. He thought I could be his guy.

That was the good part. The not-so-good part took up the rest of the letter.

I'm going to be straight with you, Jonas. Your academic record worries me. My basketball players are student-athletes, with the emphasis on *student*. There is another high school point guard with whom I'm in contact. Right now, you hold the edge on the basketball court, and I have told him so. I have also told him that he has the edge in the class-room. Before I can offer you a scholar-ship, I will need to see clear evidence that you will be able to meet the high academic standards of Monitor College.

To be specific: you will need to com-plete your current junior-year classes with a minimum 3.0 grade point average. Listed below are the classes Monitor College requires you to complete—again with a minimum 3.0 grade point average— during your senior year.
- Chemistry
- Algebra II/Trigonometry
- Language Arts
- Social Studies
- Spanish

You will also need to score at least
five hundred on each section of the SAT.
I do not need to tell you that this is a
much more difficult course of study than
you have undertaken in the past. To
succeed, you will need to put forth the
kind of effort in the classroom that you
have put forth on the basketball court.
It is up to you.

Sincerely,
Gregory Richter
Men's Head Basketball Coach
Monitor College

10

I T HAD BEEN ONE THING to talk about becoming a better student, but seeing in black-and-white Richter's list of requirements was overwhelming. In the previous weeks, I'd actually raised my hand in class a few times. The kids around me were surprised; the teachers nodded with pleasure.

But raising your hand in class a few times isn't the same as studying hard for tough classes for an entire year. Could I do that? And if I did somehow get into Monitor College, was I smart enough to succeed? What would be the point of going all the way to New England only to flunk out?

My mind went in circles for a while, until I thought of Lisa Yee. Lisa lived right down the block, and she was one of the smartest kids at Redwood High. When we were little, we'd played together at Stambaugh Park, and we were still good friends. Lisa knew all about colleges, and she also knew what I could and couldn't do. Most importantly, she'd be straight with me.

My dad wasn't home for dinner, which was typical. When we finished eating, I asked my mom if I could borrow her car, and she said yes. I took out my cell and phoned Lisa. "How about we go to Starbucks?" I asked.

"Sorry, Jonas. I've got homework."

"Come on, Lisa. You can bring your laptop. I need to talk to you."

"Why can't we just talk now, on the phone?"

"Because I have to show you something. Please, Lisa. It won't take long."

Twenty minutes later we were drinking hot chocolate at a corner table inside the Starbucks by the Redwood City train station. "So?" Lisa said, pushing her long hair back over her shoulders. "What's the big mystery?"

I unfolded Coach Richter's letter and handed it to her.

As she read, the impatience in her eyes was replaced by excitement. When she was halfway through, she reached over, took hold of my arm, and squeezed. "Jonas, this is fantastic."

"Have you heard of Monitor College?" I asked when she'd finished reading.

"No, but that doesn't mean anything," she said as she opened her laptop. "There are a thousand schools in the East I've never heard of."

I looked over her shoulder and watched as she typed *Monitor College* into the Google search box. Within seconds, she was jumping from webpage to webpage. At each stop, she found something new to like about Monitor. After about five minutes, she closed her laptop and looked at me. "It's a perfect fit for you."

"And you think I can do what Richter wants me to do?"

A quizzical look came over her face. "Is that what you wanted to talk to me about?"

I nodded. "I've never been much of a student."

"Jonas, trust me. You'll have no trouble with the SAT, and you can get Bs if you study."

I shook my head. "In some classes, yeah. But I got a D in biology last year, and I barely got a C– in geometry first semester this year. How am I going to get Bs in chemistry and Algebra II?"

Lisa's brows knit. "Okay, those will be difficult, but I'll help you. I've taken both of those classes already, so I know what you'll need to study." She reached over and squeezed my arm again. "You can do it, Jonas. I know you can."

I was feeling pumped up by Lisa's confidence in me when I opened my front door, but that feeling vanished the instant I saw my parents. They were sitting at the kitchen table, papers spread out in front of them, their faces grim. They barely looked at me as I came in.

I'd planned on showing them Richter's letter; instead, I went to my room and read it over a few more times. I'd put it away when my mom tapped on my door, opened it, and then stepped inside. She didn't usually do that — once I closed my door at night, they both left me alone.

"What happened?" I asked, even though I knew the answer.

Her eyes were sad. "Two weeks."

Neither of us said anything for a while. Then my mom smiled. "The good news is that he's going to start a new chapter in his life. He never liked that dispatch job, anyway. We're going through a rough patch, but in the long run everything will work out."

11

ONCE MY DAD LOST HIS job, coming home from school was awkward. He had no place to go and nothing to do, so he was always hanging around the house. Little by little he changed too — and not for the better. First, he stopped shaving. He's got a heavy beard, and within a week it looked wild, like the beard of a mass murderer in a horror film. Next, he stopped paying attention to his clothes. He'd wear the same old Mount Shasta sweatshirt and the same old ripped blue jeans day after day. But the worst thing was the drinking — every afternoon he'd polish off a six-pack of beer, and sometimes he drank more.

My mom was working extra hours at the hairdresser, so most afternoons and evenings, it was just my dad and me at home. We'd microwave frozen dinners and eat them with plastic knives and forks so we wouldn't have to wash up. When my mom came home, her blue eyes seemed paler and so did her skin. She hardly ate, so every day she looked thinner.

Those weeks were miserable, but one good thing did happen: I taught myself how to study. I can play basketball for hours, but after ten minutes of looking at a book, I had to fight the urge to play a video game or turn on ESPN. Slowly, though, I trained myself to concentrate.

Lisa was right about my grades, at least for history and English. By reading everything twice, checking answers, and asking questions in class, I was earning Bs. Teachers I thought I hated, like Mr. Whitten, turned out to be okay once I started acting differently.

The tough class was geometry. I'd blown off math for so long that I had all kinds of holes in my knowledge. I wasn't entirely sure what the slope of a line was and had only the haziest idea how to find it. While all my other grades were going up, my C– in geometry was drifting toward a D.

In mid-March I got myself switched to Mr. Nutting's math class. Nutting was known as a hard-ass, but he also had the reputation of helping anyone who asked. I spent lunch periods in his room working through the problem sets, slowly filling in the holes in my knowledge. Nutting was honest. "You might not be a math whiz, Jonas, but you're smart enough. Just stay with it."

With Nutting's help, my geometry grade slowly rose. I wouldn't say using the point-slope formula ever came as easily to me as shooting a free throw, but it wasn't like climbing Mount Everest, either. When I went online to check my grades after quarter finals, I had a B– in geometry and a B or better in everything else.

12

TOOK THE SAT AT SCHOOL one afternoon. Lisa had been right — it wasn't that hard. When I got home that day, I spotted a Lexus with a Hertz rental car license frame in our driveway. When I opened the front door, I saw a strange man sitting across the kitchen table from my dad. They were deep in conversation. I looked, and then looked again. It was my uncle Frank.

If you look at photos of Uncle Frank and my dad from when they were in high school, you can see immediately that they're brothers, and it's hard to tell who is older. That makes sense because they were born only eighteen months apart. But sitting across from one another at the kitchen table that day, they didn't look like brothers — and they didn't look the same age.

My dad had started working at the sand and gravel company right out of high school, but Uncle Frank went to the University of Washington, where he earned a business degree. Uncle Frank now owns about twenty fancy hamburger places up in Seattle. The Blue Jay restaurants have made him rich — millionaire rich.

Uncle Frank looked like he could have been my older brother.

His face was smooth, his blond hair perfectly combed, and his clothes crisply pressed. He was gym-club muscular and had what looked like a diamond ring on his little finger. My dad — with his sweatshirt, stubble, and extra forty pounds — looked ten years older.

Uncle Frank smiled when he saw me, came out to the living room, and shook my hand as if I were an adult. "You have really grown, Jonas. How long has it been since I've seen you? It must be four years."

"Good to see you, Uncle Frank," I said, embarrassed and confused. Why was he visiting now?

We both stood awkwardly, neither of us knowing what to say next. Then my dad's voice came from the kitchen. "Your uncle Frank and I have some business to talk over, Jonas. We'll all go out to dinner later when your mom comes home."

I went into the den and turned on the television, but I kept the sound low so I could hear what they were saying. Uncle Frank did all the talking. I couldn't follow everything he said, but I picked up stray sentences here and there. *Right now the place is failing . . . Sure you could . . . You'd be doing me the favor . . . I'm going to have to move on this soon.*

My mom came home a little later, and we went to dinner at a fancy restaurant up in Woodside. It was the first time in a long while that we'd gone anywhere. Uncle Frank ordered a couple of bottles of wine and then told stories about how great Seattle was. "There are mountains and lakes, golf courses and ski resorts. It's got everything, including rain. You'd love it up there, Jonas." My mom was smiling and talked some, but my dad stayed mostly quiet all through the evening. When the bill came, Uncle Frank insisted on paying. I could tell my dad didn't like that, but he let him.

Uncle Frank left early the next morning. Once he was gone, my dad explained. "He's offered me a job. He wants me to manage one of his restaurants up in Seattle."

"You? Manage a restaurant?" I said, without thinking. "Could you do that?"

My father laughed. "That's exactly what I said to him. He seems to think I can."

My head was spinning. All that talk about how much I'd love Seattle suddenly made sense. "That's great," I said, forcing the words out.

My dad shrugged. "It is and it isn't. I'll have a job, but if we moved to Seattle, you'd have to start over with new teachers, a new coach, and new teammates. I don't want to ruin your chance for that scholarship, especially since I'm not sure I can even do the work. So this is your call."

I sat absolutely still. He'd said exactly what I'd been thinking.

A long moment passed. Then he picked up his glass and drank some of his beer. "You don't have to decide now, Jonas," he said as he put his glass down. "Tomorrow or the next day is fine. Frank can wait that long."

"No," I said, and my voice sounded strange to me. "I don't need to think about it. Guys transfer to new schools all the time. It'll be okay."

"You're sure?"

"I'm sure," I insisted, even though I wasn't sure at all.

The next day was May 10 — my seventeenth birthday. When I came home from school, a For Sale sign was in front of the house.

13

O NCE MY DAD KNEW HE'D be working again, he shaved and changed his clothes every day. Instead of drinking beer in front of the television, he spent his afternoons at the kitchen table reading library books on restaurant management. My mom's eyes regained their normal blue color, and the worry was gone from them. She still worked extra hours, but she was eating more. Our situations had reversed. Now I was the one who had trouble eating; now I was the one who was afraid of the future.

I had school every day and homework every night and final exams coming up fast. I had Coach Russell telling me that I would do fine in Seattle, and Mr. Nutting telling me that if I studied hard I could pass Algebra II, and Lisa telling me that chemistry was more memorization than anything else.

The thing that kept me from going crazy with worry was basketball. I was playing on a spring rec league team that had two games a week. Rec basketball was far easier on the mind than high school ball. Our coach just rolled the ball onto the floor and let us play. Only a few parents bothered to attend the games, which was great.

I wanted to go into a time bubble, where I could just play on that rec league team forever. But in early June, during one crazy-long Saturday of pure basketball pleasure, my team played from noon until ten at night and won the league tournament. In the locker room after the game, our coach gave me a plastic trophy with the letters MVP on the base. My teammates cheered for me, and then — exhausted — I headed out the gym door and back home. Spring basketball was over, and that meant the school year would soon be coming to a close too.

Through that whole time, the For Sale sign had hung from a post hammered into the front lawn. In a strange way, I liked the sign. If the house never sold, then we'd never leave. But when I came home on the Wednesday of finals week, I saw my dad and mom on the porch shaking hands with their realtor. I looked to the post: the For Sale sign was still up, but now the word *Sold* ran diagonally across it.

My parents smiled all through dinner that night, talking excitedly about Seattle and the Blue Jay restaurant my dad was going to manage. I forced myself to smile too, even though a fist-size lump filled my throat.

During lunch on the last day of school, Mark tried to cheer me up. "Seattle's not so far," he said, as he bit into his hamburger. "I could drive up and visit you, or you could come down and stay with us. It's not like you're going to the moon." After school Lisa and I walked home together. "We can keep up with each other on Facebook," she said. "We've known each other since before kindergarten. We've got to stay in touch."

That night I lay on my bed in the darkness, unable to sleep. As the cars passed by on the street outside, the shadows created by their headlights danced across the ceiling of my room. My life was being cut up into a thousand pieces, and those pieces were being thrown up into the air. I was going to have to prove myself all over again.

It was late when I finally fell asleep. I woke up when my dad knocked hard on the door. "Rise and shine, Jonas. The moving guys will be coming in two days. We've got packing to do."

PART TWO

1

ON THE MORNING OF JULY 1, I was standing in front of our new home, an old house in the Tangletown neighborhood of Seattle. Mom was down in Redwood City closing bank accounts, so in Seattle it was just my dad and me.

Two musclebound gorillas were unloading our stuff. Because of his leg and his back, my dad couldn't help, which drove him crazy. When he barked out instructions, the moving guys would grunt and keep doing what they were doing.

At first I'd stationed myself inside the house, but every place I went, the moving men followed. I'd grinned stupidly at them, but they'd scowled back. "Where's this go?" they'd ask, their giant tattooed arms holding a chair or a box or a cabinet.

"I guess right there is good."

Thump.

Then my father would rush in. "Not there," he'd say, and he'd make them take it down to the basement or into the living room. They'd pick up whatever it was, glare at me, and grumble their way to the new spot.

I moved to the sidewalk, where the moving guys couldn't

glower at me. But I felt stupid standing around where neighbors could see me.

I was feeling completely lost when I spotted a tall, sandy-haired kid, hands in his pockets, looking at me from across the street. I could tell from his face — some nasty zits and the beginning of a beard — that he was about my age.

Whenever I glanced at him, he dropped his head and stared at the ground. My dad noticed. "Invite him over, Jonas. He could be your new best friend."

"If he wants to come over, he'll come over."

My dad looked at him, then at me, then back at him. Next, without any warning, he called out. "Hey, kid, come over here and meet my son."

"What are you doing, Dad?" I hissed.

"I'm being neighborly, which is what you should be."

2

HE KID'S HEAD STAYED DOWN as he shuffled over. "I'm Robert Dolan," my dad said, sticking out his hand. Then he motioned to me. "This is my son, Jonas. My wife, Mary, is back with our old house in California. She'll be joining us soon."

The kid barely looked up. "I'm Levi Rawdon," he answered in a voice strangely soft for such a big guy.

"You live near here, Levi?" my dad asked.

"There," the kid said, and he pointed down the block. "The brown house."

I looked to where he was pointing. Our rental house was okay. It had two stories, the beige paint wasn't peeling, the lawn was green, and the bushes in the flower beds were alive. Levi's house was both beat-up and small—only one story—with peeling paint, no flowers at all, and kids' bikes strewn around the front yard.

At that moment, one of the moving guys dropped a box from the back of the truck onto the street. The crash was loud—like two cars hitting.

My dad's spine straightened as he rushed forward. The ape stepped aside, but as he did he glared at my dad, daring him to make a big deal out of it. My dad glared right back, then knelt down and ripped the tape off the box so he could peer inside. I knew what he was afraid of: one of the boxes contained Irish plates that my mom had gotten when her own mother had died. They were the only things she had from her parents.

For thirty seconds, my dad's hands waded through the box. Finally, he stood and looked the moving guy square in the eye. "All pots and pans. Nothing broken. You were lucky." The big guy snorted, picked up the box, and carried it up the porch stairs and into the kitchen.

I turned back to Levi. "Have you lived here all your life?"

Levi shook his head. "I was born in Arkansas. We came to Seattle three years ago — my parents and my four sisters and me." He paused. "Do you have any brothers or sisters?"

"No," I answered.

Levi's eyes looked toward the movers again as they climbed the porch stairs, boxes in hand. "My father thought about renting that house, only it cost too much."

We were a long way from being rich, but my dad had said the rent for the house was way less than it would have been in California. I glanced again at Levi's tiny house and imagined his big family jammed in there. Where did they all sleep? When I looked back, I caught him staring at my house, his eyes moving from the ground floor to the upstairs. He was probably wondering what three people would do with so much room.

"I played basketball for my high school in California," I said, just to say something. "How about you? Do you play?" It was a risky question because he looked like he might be one of those tall guys who aren't coordinated enough to tie their own shoes. Guys like that hate to be asked about basketball, but I got lucky.

"Yeah, I play forward for Harding High."

"You play for Harding? I just registered at Harding this morning."

Levi beamed. "That's great. We'll be teammates."

As soon as I'd mentioned basketball, he morphed into another person. The slouch disappeared, and he stood with his shoulders straight. He had a broad forehead, dark brown eyes, a straight nose, thick lips, and a strong jaw. He was bigger than I'd thought, probably six five or six six, and more muscular.

Once I discovered he was on the Harding High team, questions jumped into my mind. *Did Harding have a point guard? Could the guy shoot? Could he pass? Could he run a fast break? Did I have a chance to beat him out for the starting spot?* I didn't ask Levi any of them. I didn't know him well enough, not then. Besides, I was afraid of what the answers might be.

There was a long moment of silence. "You must also play football," I said, scrambling for another topic. "Tight end? Linebacker? Quarterback?"

Levi's mouth turned down, and he shook his head. "I won't play football. It's a sin to hurt another human being on purpose."

"A sin?" I asked, not sure I'd heard correctly.

"Yes. A sin."

Was he joking? What kid ever talked about sin? I nearly laughed, but I caught myself. I'm glad I did, because if Levi thought I was laughing at religion — at God — he'd have gone back into that squashed house of his, and I'd have never known him. I'd have played on the Harding High team with him; but I wouldn't have *known* him. At the end, everything went wrong. But knowing Levi — being his best friend — that had been right.

3

I SPENT THE NEXT TWO DAYS working around the house. There were boxes to unload, carpets to unroll, furniture to move. On July 4 my dad and I went out for pizza before driving to Sea-Tac Airport to pick up my mom. From the freeway I could see fireworks exploding over Lake Union.

My mom's flight was late, and she'd been stuck next to some guy who reeked of cigarettes, ate beef jerky, and hacked away for two hours. She was in no mood to talk — still, I was glad she was finally in Seattle.

When I awoke the following morning, I saw Mount Rainier out my window for the first time — clouds had covered it up until then. I'd known it was there, but I hadn't known it was so enormous. The mountain rose like a giant coming out of the earth.

Downstairs, I found a note on the kitchen table from my mom saying that she and my dad wouldn't be back until dinner. I fried myself a couple of eggs with bacon, grabbed my basketball, and headed out. Because I'd heard how cold and rainy Seattle is, I put on a hooded sweatshirt, but the sun was bright in the sky.

I knew from doing an Internet search that there were serious high school pickup games at the Green Lake Community Center.

I'd need to play there eventually, but I hadn't shot a basketball in a week, and I wanted to have my A game when I took on Seattle's best players.

So instead of Green Lake, I headed to the Good Shepherd Center, a nearby park that I'd found using Google Maps. The streets wound this way and that — Tangletown is called Tangletown for a reason — but I finally found it.

The basketball hoops were tucked behind a brick building that had been a school before being converted into an arts center. The backboards were small, but the rims were straight and had nylon nets.

For an hour I practiced my stutter step, my crossover, and my jump shot. Then, I shot fifty free throws, sinking forty-one. After the last shot — a swish — dropped through, I retrieved the ball and held it, wondering what to do next.

That's when I heard the *thump-thump-thump* of a basketball being dribbled. The brick building blocked my view, but the dribbling came closer and closer until finally the guy with the basketball turned a corner and I could see him.

Levi Rawdon.

He looked startled for a moment; then he smiled broadly and waved. "Jonas," he called out.

"Hey, Levi," I called back.

As he approached, I felt oddly confused. I needed to make friends, and what better place to start than with someone who lived on my block and was on the Harding High basketball team? But that stuff about sin made me wish that someone else had rounded that corner. If I swore or I said something nasty about somebody, I didn't want the guy looking at me like I was on an express train to hell.

We shot around for a while, but shooting around gets old fast. Levi was six inches taller and thirty pounds heavier. Still, if you don't challenge yourself, you don't get better. The other kid that Coach Richter was considering was playing against somebody, somewhere. "Game to eleven?" I asked. "Winner's outs. Okay?"

4

COULDN'T MATCH UP AGAINST LEVI physically, but if you know your strengths and exploit your opponent's weaknesses, you can win games you should lose. If I knocked down a few jump shots early in the game, he'd be forced to guard me closely. Once he got in my face, I'd out-quick him to the hoop.

Defending him would be tougher. If he was determined to muscle me, backing in and backing in, I'd have no chance. That style of play is boring, though, and I was pretty sure Levi would want a decent game. Whenever he dribbled, I'd go for the steal. I've got quick hands, so I figured I could force some turnovers.

The strategy was sound, and in Redwood City I'd used it to beat guys bigger than me. Only it turned out that Levi wasn't like the forwards I'd played against in California. Shooting around with him, I'd sensed he was pretty quick for six six. Playing against him, I discovered he wasn't pretty quick; he was leopard quick.

I had no chance.

If I backed off him when he had the ball, he could shoot over me; but if I got in his face, he could power to the hoop. When I was on offense, he could get right up on me because I wasn't quick enough to drive by him. Shooting over the top of a guy six inches taller was hopeless. On TV I saw Bill Nye the Science Guy use a small knife to touch mercury, saying that it was both a solid and a liquid. Levi played like he was both solid and liquid.

I couldn't let him crush me like a bug, so I resorted to pushing and grabbing. I kept waiting for him to stick a shoulder into me and put me on my butt, but he just played through all my fouls. Five straight times he beat me, in spite of the fouls I laid on him.

By the time we'd finished our fifth game, I was hungry and thirsty. Still, my pride wouldn't let me go home until I'd won at something. "How about a game of Horse?"

Finally I had him. Any kind of trick shot and Levi was lost. Shooting from behind the backboard, shooting underhanded with my back to the basket, bouncing the ball off the ground and then into the basket — all that garbagey, fun stuff that every kid does, Levi hadn't done. I destroyed him in Horse three times.

Before we headed back, there was one thing I wanted to see. "Dunk for me," I said. "I want to see what you've got."

He shrugged, backed up, loped down the lane, soared above the hoop, and then brought down the wimpiest dunk I'd ever seen.

"Come on, Levi. Jam it like you mean it, like you would in a game."

Levi frowned. "Coach Knecht doesn't let us dunk. He says it's showboating."

"Well, Coach Knecht isn't here now. So do it for me, your new friend." It was a dumb thing to say, but from the start I sensed that Levi would do anything for anybody if it was in the name of friendship.

He backed up to half-court again, but this time he came like a tornado. He took off just inside the free-throw line and raised the ball — cupped in his huge hand — above his head, his arm fully extended. He seemed to hang suspended in midair, but then the ball came down, a powerful tomahawk jam that left me slack-jawed. I stared at the rocking backboard for a while before I looked back at Levi. His eyes were wide open; he seemed as amazed by what he'd done as I was.

On the walk home, I asked if he'd made all-league.

"No."

So then I asked him if he was the leading scorer on the team.

"No."

"Second leading scorer?"

"No."

"What does your coach have you do?"

"Rebound and set screens."

"He doesn't run any plays for you?"

"No."

I shook my head. "I'm telling you, Levi, if you were on my team in California, Coach Russell would run the offense through you. Knecht doesn't know what he's doing."

Levi didn't say anything, but his eyes flashed with anger. It was the first time I'd seen him angry.

5

EVERY AFTERNOON FOR THE NEXT week, Levi and I played basketball at the Good Shepherd Center. I would have gone straight to the courts, but when I knocked on his front door, Levi always asked me in.

Stepping inside his house was like entering a different world. Religion was everywhere. Above the front door was a sign that read: THIS FAMILY BELIEVES. Over the back of a beat-up rocking chair was a blanket with a design that showed three stark crosses on the top of a barren hill. Written on the blanket, in old-fashioned lettering, were the words: *An emblem of suffering and shame.* All of the rooms had a cross on the wall, and the only book I ever saw in the house was a Bible.

The place was dark and messy, with too much stuff crammed into too little space. Two of Levi's sisters must have slept in the front room because two mattresses were leaning against a wall in the corner. The worst thing, though, was the smell — a mixture of cooked ground beef and dirty towels.

The one room that didn't fit the house was Levi's bedroom. My room isn't a sty, but there's usually a pile of dirty clothes in a corner, a *Sports Illustrated* open on my bed, and some stray papers on my desk or on the floor by the trash can.

Levi's bed was perfectly made; his tiny desk was completely clear of clutter; there wasn't a scrap of paper on the floor. His walls were bare—I don't think there was even a pushpin hole anywhere. One day he opened a drawer to get a sweatshirt. He had only four shirts, but each was perfectly folded as if it were about to be displayed on a table at Nordstrom.

Levi's mother was a tiny woman with dull eyes and dull red hair pulled back into a short ponytail. She always said hello to me in a weirdly hollow voice before going into the kitchen to mop the floor or wash dishes. His father wasn't around much, which was fine with me. He was a bear of a man, with wild eyebrows, gray-black wiry hair, and fierce black eyes.

Levi had a mob of younger sisters. Rachel, the oldest, was fifteen. She was a goddess—a tall blonde with sky blue eyes and a body that made me look at my shoes so I wouldn't stare. One time, with me standing there, Levi's dad yelled at Rachel, telling her that her shirt was too tight. "Go back to your room and change your clothes. A woman who creates lust in the heart of a man is sinful." Rachel's mouth twisted in anger, but when she left two minutes later, she was wearing an oversize UW T-shirt.

Levi's other sisters were much younger than Rachel. They followed him around, tugging on his shirt. Before we could go to the basketball court, he'd have to take them into the backyard and swing each of them in a wide circle, while they laughed and laughed. To speed things up, a couple of times I offered to swing Maddie, the youngest of the girls. She let me, and she said thanks when I stopped, but she wasn't satisfied until Levi had twirled her.

Eventually Levi would break from his little sisters, and we would leave his house. Then, it was a ten-minute walk to the Good Shepherd Center, where we'd go one-on-one. Occasionally I'd catch fire and beat him, but 90 percent of the time he shut me down. When we were exhausted, we'd play a handful of games of Horse, and then I'd beat him every time. I'd like to say that evened things up, but Horse is just Horse.

6

AFTER A COUPLE OF HOURS of basketball, we'd get a drink of water and then sit on the grass and talk. Levi told me that back in Arkansas he'd hunted and fished and hiked and basically lived outdoors as much as he could. As he described his life in the mountains, I kept thinking of the kid in *Where the Red Fern Grows*. When I asked him why his family had moved, his face soured. "There are meth houses up in the mountains. My dad tried to bring the word of God to the people who lived there, but they wouldn't listen. After the police arrested one family, my dad said it wasn't safe for us to stay. He packed us up in a day, and then we were gone."

His father had been a minister in Arkansas for eighteen years. He wanted to be a minister again, but it was hard to establish a new church in a new city. During the week, his father worked as a mechanic at a Ford dealership, but on Sunday he preached in a rented room at the Phinney Ridge Community Center. Levi said that slowly the number of people attending had grown, so that now about forty people were at the service every week. "Last January my dad signed a lease for a store on Kenwood Place, and we're turning it into a church. When we finish, Dad will go back to preaching God's word full-time."

I'm not much of a talker, but Levi had been so open with me that I had to tell him a little about why we'd moved to Seattle. Once I'd started, something about him made it easy to keep talking, so I ended up telling him not only about my dad losing his job, but also about my hope for a scholarship to Monitor College.

Then we talked hoops. I'd done an Internet search on Harding's basketball team, so I knew their leading scorer was a long-faced black kid named Cash Washington, and that their point guard was Donny Brindle, a white guy who'd averaged six points and four assists a game. I wanted to ask Levi questions about Brindle's weaknesses, but Levi wasn't the kind of person who'd run down a teammate, and I wouldn't have wanted him to anyway. So instead I tried to get a feel for the coach.

"Coach Knecht is a good man."

"Sure, sure. But tell me about him. Young? Old? Tough? Easy-going?"

"He's old, and he's got arthritis in his back, which makes him bent over. But he's tough. You play solid defense for Mr. Knecht or you don't play."

"What about the offense? Does he have you run set plays or do you freelance?"

Levi shook his head. "Not much freelancing. We're structured on offense."

I didn't like the sound of that. Coach Russell ran a freewheeling, fast-breaking offense. "But you fast break sometimes, right?"

"Sure, but only if we have the numbers and a clear path to the hoop."

That night, watching television, I chewed on what Levi had said. I'd never played at a slow tempo, and Brindle had three years' experience running Knecht's offense. How could I beat him out for the starting spot? And if I couldn't beat him out, what chance did I have to impress Coach Richter?

7

OING ONE-ON-ONE AGAINST LEVI WAS okay, but by the middle of July, I was itching for more. My game is seeing the court, making passes, running a team. I needed to play five-on-five, full-court basketball.

"I read online that there are good pickup games at Green Lake," I said to Levi one Tuesday during a break. "Do any Harding guys go there?"

"Donny Brindle plays on a select team in the summer, but some Harding guys are probably there."

"Maybe we could go to Green Lake tomorrow."

"All right," Levi said, sounding like he was making an appointment with the dentist to get a tooth pulled.

For the rest of the afternoon, he was a step slow. I beat him three straight games — and I'd never done that. Something was definitely up with Green Lake.

"We don't have to change anything," I said on the walk home. "We can keep playing one-on-one at the Good Shepherd Center."

"No, we'll go to Green Lake. Coach Knecht would want us there."

⊛ ⊛ ⊛

When I stopped by Levi's house the next day, he was lying on the floor playing Candy Land with his three little sisters. I was eager to get going, but he had me help Maddie move her marker around the board. When the game ended, he hugged each girl a couple of times and told all of them that they were princesses. I didn't think we were ever going to leave, but finally we made it out the door. It was a full hour after I'd left my house before I finally pushed open the door of the gym at the Green Lake Community Center and stepped inside.

Immediately I loved the place. Old hardwood floors, exposed wood beams, and close walls — you could just feel the thousands of games that had been played there.

I wanted to take a minute to soak up the atmosphere, but before we had taken three steps, a tall black kid called out: "Hey, it's Dumb-Dumb!" Immediately Levi looked over at me, his face reddening.

Then they were all around him. Three guys. I recognized the tall, wiry black kid — Cash Washington. I wasn't sure of the names of the other two — a stocky black guy and a red-haired kid with bad acne. All three punched Levi on the shoulder, shook him this way and that. "Good to see you, Double D. Where you been hiding?" the stocky kid said.

The whole thing had a weird feel. They called him "Dumb-Dumb," yet they liked him. I could see it in their eyes, hear it in their voices. Eventually the redhead guy with the zits nodded toward me. "Who's your buddy, Double D?"

I stepped forward. "Jonas Dolan. I'm going to Harding in the fall."

"Hey, Jonas," each said in turn, bumping knuckles with me as they introduced themselves. The muscular black guy with the cornrows was DeShawn Lewis, and the acned redhead was Nick Masar. Cash told me his name last, and I pretended it was new to me. Everybody was all smiles, but they were sizing me up. How quick was I? How well did I shoot? What kind of defense did I play?

We shot around on a side court, waiting for a chance to play on the main court. As we warmed up, the other guys asked Levi what he'd been doing and why he hadn't been to the gym until now. Nick and DeShawn continued calling Levi "Double D," which is better than "Dumb-Dumb," but not by much. Cash always used "Dumb-Dumb."

Finally it was our turn to play. "Can you handle the ball?" Cash asked me as we stepped on the court.

"I started at point guard for my team last year."

"Okay. You take the point. Just remember, I'm the scorer on this team; everything goes through me. Understand?"

8

UNDERSTOOD. AND I DID IT, even though I didn't like it. I'd bring the ball into frontcourt; somebody would set a screen; Cash would come off it; I'd feed him the ball; he'd shoot. Our variety—if you could call it that—came from where the screen was set and who set it. Sometimes it was Nick on the right side, sometimes DeShawn on the left, and sometimes Levi at the top of the key.

Cash was on fire early, and we jumped out to a 6–3 lead. But once our opponents figured out that Cash was our whole show, they double-teamed him. Instead of passing out of the double team, Cash forced up bad shots, and we ended up losing, 11–8.

We trudged to the sideline, waiting our next turn. We got lucky when one team disbanded, but it was still a long time before we were back on the main court.

In the second game, our opponents double-teamed Cash from the start. Cash drained a couple of amazing jump shots to keep us close, but little by little the game was slipping away.

I hate to lose, and I hate even more having to sit around waiting to play. So, with the score 7–4 in their favor, I faked a pass to Cash coming off the screen and instead fed the ball to DeShawn.

DeShawn bobbled the pass for an instant, but then gathered himself and drove to the hoop for a lay-up. After that I shared the ball, setting up everybody for shots, not just Cash.

The game turned around.

A ball hog is tough on everybody. It gets old running up and down the court without ever having a chance to shine. Some guys can give 100 percent anyway—Levi was like that—but most players can't. Once I started feeding Nick and DeShawn, they stepped up their games. If Cash was open and I fed someone else, he would clap his hands and scowl. But we won, so how much griping could he do?

It wasn't just that game that we won. Once I started moving the ball around, we dominated the court, winning three straight. We finally lost, but only because we were so tired that we couldn't make our legs move.

That defeat ended the afternoon. Levi and I headed back to Tangletown, with me asking Levi about the guys on the other Green Lake teams and Levi telling me that most of them played for Ballard or Nathan Hale or Ingraham. "All those schools are in our league."

"And we took it to them," I said, whacking him on the shoulder. "We ate their lunches."

Then we both fell quiet. I could sense that he was thinking the same thing I was thinking. Finally I spoke. "What was all that 'Double D' stuff?"

His mouth twisted and he looked away. "My classes in Arkansas weren't any good, but I'm lousy at school anyway. Last year I flunked two classes, so I couldn't play the last month of the season. The guys razz me about it, but they don't mean anything."

We talked about other things, and then split apart. Back in my own house, I made myself a ham and cheese sandwich, stuck it on a plate with a half-dozen Oreos, grabbed a carton of milk and an apple, and carried it all into the backyard. I ate in a big chair in the center of the yard, the sun shining down on me, a breeze cooling the air. Once I'd finished eating, I closed my eyes and soaked up the rays.

Pictures started flickering through my mind, like the slides in a PowerPoint. I saw Levi playing Candy Land with his little sisters, his eyes fixed on the next card in the draw. I saw him in his backyard twirling the girls by their arms, the smile on his face as broad as the smile on theirs. I remembered the way Rachel looked at him, as if she were the older sister and he were a nerdy younger brother.

Something was different about Levi. *Dumb* is a cruel word, and it was the wrong word, and *Dumb-Dumb* was doubly cruel and doubly wrong. But what was the right word? Telling me that tackling someone was a sin . . . insisting on always calling Knecht *Mr.* Knecht or *Coach* Knecht . . . playing board games on the floor like a child.

Simple.

Maybe that was the right word.

Levi was simple, like a child. It was the best thing about him, and it was the worst, too.

9

AFTER THAT, WE PLAYED FULL-COURT basketball every day at Green Lake. They were pickup games, but they were hard fought. We won more than we lost, which made everybody happy except Cash, who always wanted the ball more. Neither Cash nor I said anything, but we both felt the tension simmering.

And then it boiled over.

We were losing 10–9 to some Ballard High guys in our last game of the day. They missed a shot, Levi rebounded, hit me with a great outlet pass, and the fast break was on. I drove the middle; Cash filled the lane on my left; Nick was racing up on my right.

My guy held his position, forcing me to pass. I faked to Cash and then delivered the ball to Nick. But my pass was a little too hard, and Nick fumbled it out-of-bounds. The Ballard guys inbounded quickly, pushed the ball up the court, and their best player hit a jump shot from the free-throw line to seal their victory and send us home as losers.

Cash glared at me as we walked off. I could read his eyes: *You should have passed to me.* He was right — he had stronger hands and the cold blood of a scorer, but instead of apologizing, I stared right back.

I want to say he looked away first, but it was me. Some guys are like that; you just can't stare them down. I headed to the water fountain to get away from him, but there was no escaping his voice. I heard him talking about how he and Nick and DeShawn were going to Golden Gardens beach to meet some hot girls. "Come with us Double D," Nick said. "Carolyn Murphy will be there. She likes you, you know."

I turned around to hear Levi say. "I have to help my mother."

Cash shook his head. "Hanging out with your momma when you could be with a girl whose body is almost as hot as the body of that sister of yours — Dumb-Dumb, you really are dumb."

Levi paled; the other guys snickered.

"Don't talk trash about his sister," I snapped. "And stop calling him Dumb-Dumb." My voice was shaky and my body was trembling. I was ready to fight, if that's what it came to.

Cash looked at me, and then turned to Levi, a mean smile on his face. "Dumb-Dumb, you don't care if I call you Dumb-Dumb, do you?"

"I care," I said, not waiting for Levi to answer.

Cash's eyes flashed. "Was I talking to you, Joan-ass? I don't think so."

My hands clenched into fists; his did the same. That's when Levi stepped between us. "It is okay, Jonas," he said, pushing me back. "I don't mind. Really, I don't. He doesn't mean anything. He's just joking around."

Cash's face relaxed, and a smug I-told-you-so smile came to his lips. I raged inside, but before I could say or do anything,

Cash strode off, Nick and DeShawn in tow. When they reached the door, Cash turned back. "See you tomorrow, Leeeeeee-vi."

As we walked home, neither of us said anything about Cash or the near fight. When he reached his house, Levi stopped. "It's my birthday today," he said. "I'm seventeen."

I smiled and pretended to punch him in the stomach. "Happy birthday. You doing anything special?"

He shook his head. "No, my dad doesn't believe in celebrating birthdays much. We'll just have dinner." With that, he turned and disappeared into his beater house.

That night my grades from Redwood High finally arrived in the mail — nearly a month late. I had an A in printmaking, a C+ in geometry, and Bs in everything else. My SAT scores had come in a week earlier, and they were fine. I e-mailed Coach Richter. Five minutes after I hit Send his answer came.

"Those are two big steps in the right direction, Jonas. Keep it up. Coach R."

10

PART OF ME WANTED TO stay away from Green Lake, but that would have been a coward's move. So Levi and I showed up the next day at the regular time. Cash and the other two guys were already there. Cash nodded at me, and then said: "How you doing, Double D?" It wasn't an accident; for the whole time we shot around waiting for a court, he never once used "Dumb-Dumb."

"Double D" wasn't great, but it wasn't as vicious as "Dumb-Dumb." People could hear "Double D" and not know what the nickname meant. Maybe I should have pushed harder with Cash — with all of them — but I didn't. Cash had backed off, so I backed off. Our truce carried over to the court too. That day I made sure I got him the ball when he was open. The guy did have good hands and a shooter's touch, even if he was a jerk.

Cash and Nick and DeShawn left early — they were headed back to the beach and the girls. When they were gone, Levi and I found a side court and shot hoops, neither of us ready to go home. We'd been shooting for a couple of minutes when a twenty-something guy wearing a muscle T-shirt stepped onto the court. "Mind if I join you?" he asked. "Name is Ryan. Ryan Hartwell."

Right away I knew he was — or had been — a basketball player. He was taller than me, but not as tall as Levi. He had sky blue eyes, dark brown hair, and just the hint of a beard. He'd clearly spent some time pumping iron, but he'd built basketball muscles, not weightlifter muscles. He looked lean and strong.

We told him our names and then went back to shooting. Hartwell had spring in his step and could knock down jumpers. He was cocky too, with the way he almost palmed the ball when he dribbled and the *What else would you expect?* look he got on his face when he swished a long jumper.

We shared the ball for five minutes or so. It felt awkward shooting with a guy that much older, so I didn't say much. Then, after I'd missed a long shot, Hartwell grabbed the rebound and held it. "I don't want to push in where I'm not wanted," he said, "but I've been watching your games these past few days. You're good players, but there are some times — especially with the pick and roll — when your positioning is off. I could help if you'd like."

I glanced at Levi. In that split second, Hartwell dribbled once and then fired up a twenty-foot jumper. His effortless release resulted in a perfect swish. I looked at Levi, and he nodded. "If you've got something to teach us," I said, "we're ready to learn."

Hartwell started with basic plays — pick and roll, pick and pop — but then he'd show us subtle variations, stepping in to take one of our places when he needed to make a point. "Plant your foot hard before you go up for a jumper. Do that and you won't drift. How high you jump is unimportant. Great shooters release the ball before the guys guarding them know they're even thinking about shooting — fast like a hummingbird."

Eventually Levi and I wore down. Hartwell noticed, and he nodded toward the drinking fountain. A few minutes later, we were sprawled out on the gym floor, too tired to go home.

"Did I hear you say you're Harding guys?" Hartwell said.

I nodded toward Levi. "He plays for Harding. I just moved to Seattle, but I started for my high school in California, and I'm hoping to play for Harding too."

Hartwell questioned Levi about his family, and Levi recited stuff I already knew. Then Hartwell looked back to me. "What city in California are you from?"

"Redwood City. It's south of San Francisco."

"Oh, yeah, I know where that is. My college roommate was from Palo Alto. Did your parents work for Apple or Google or one of those high-tech firms?"

I laughed. "No way."

Hartwell smiled. "So you're not a billionaire's son?"

"Not even close."

Silence followed, and then Levi stood. "I've got to get home," he said.

I climbed to my feet and followed him. As we were leaving the gym, I called back to Hartwell. "Hey, are you a coach?"

"Not yet," he said. "But someday."

11

EVEN BEFORE ALL THE MOVING boxes were unpacked, my dad had started working at the Blue Jay restaurant in the Northgate Mall. He left the house each day around noon and didn't return home until after midnight. You'd think that much work would wear him out, but on the rare times when I did see him, he looked better. He was losing weight, his eyes were alive, and the recycling bin wasn't filled with empty beer bottles.

My mom was hired at Great Clips in Greenwood, a hair salon that was close to the house. She was working part-time, but she said that she was sure it would go to full-time in a matter of months. I wanted a job too, but when I'd asked my dad about working for him at the Blue Jay, he'd screwed up his face. "I can't hire you, Jonas. The other workers will see you as some sort of spy, and I need them to trust me. But here's what I can do. This house needs a lot of work. I won't have time to do any of it, so I'll pay you a buck over minimum wage to work for me. The first thing on the list is clearing out the weeds from the flower beds. What do you say?"

I agreed to work for him, and I drifted into a good routine. I'd get up late, eat a little breakfast, and then kill the morning doing nothing. After an early lunch, I'd stop by Levi's house. We'd walk down to Green Lake, hook up with the Harding guys, and play until three. I'd hustle home, eat something fast, and then work in the yard or paint or clean something—whatever my dad had laid out for me. Then it was a shower, another meal—either with my mom or alone—and up to my room. I'd log on to Facebook to check for messages from Lisa Yee or Mark Westwood. Or I'd play Halo or watch a baseball game on the computer. A couple of times I asked Levi if he wanted to catch a movie somewhere, but both times he said no. Maybe movies were against his religion, or maybe he didn't have any money.

Ryan Hartwell would sit up in the stands every day and watch our games, shouting out encouragement. If we lost, he'd come down and shoot around with us on a side court. He worked mainly with Levi and me, but he spent time with Cash and the other guys too. I never saw him spend any time with guys from the other high schools. That puzzled me then, but now I get it. Nothing Hartwell did was by accident.

During our sessions on the side court, Hartwell taught Levi how to do a reverse jam, how to go up and under, how to pinwheel the ball down. "A rim-rattling dunk intimidates an opponent," Hartwell said. He paused, and a smile came to his face. His eyes took in both of us. "Get a little swagger in your game, and other teams will back off. Even the refs will back off. If you play it right, you can make the rules."

Levi picked up Hartwell's lessons quickly, and both Hartwell and I tried to get him to dunk more in the actual games. Every once in a while, Levi would throw one down, but not often. It was as if he was afraid that at any minute Coach Knecht would come bursting through the doors of the gym and yell at him to knock it off. The fun parts of basketball — of anything — made Levi uncomfortable.

One afternoon, as we were shooting around after Cash and the other guys had left, I told Hartwell about my hopes for a basketball scholarship to Monitor College. He'd gone to college somewhere in the East, and he grew interested as I spoke. "I've never actually been to Monitor College," he said, "but I've heard nothing but good things about it. You keep playing hard, and you'll get that scholarship. I played Division Two college ball myself, and you've got enough game. Trust me — I know."

Hartwell's words gave my confidence a huge boost. Still, who knew if I'd even get enough playing time to show Richter what I could do? I needed to see Brindle play the point so I could measure myself against him, but that matchup was months away.

12

TOWARD THE END OF AUGUST, Cash went to St. Louis to visit his brother, and Nick took off for Missoula to visit grandparents. I don't know if DeShawn went anywhere, but he stopped coming. Guys from other teams were also gone, so the games at Green Lake became raggedy. Levi and I kept going because we had nothing else to do.

When I returned home one afternoon, an eight-year-old Subaru Outback, a little scraped and a little dented, sat in the driveway. My mom's new car didn't look like much, but my dad said it was mechanically sound. "I'll need it for work sometimes," my mom said, "but you'll be able to use it quite a bit. In fact, why don't you take it and go camping up in the mountains this weekend? Ask your friend Levi. School starts soon, and you haven't had any sort of vacation."

Levi and I left two days later. He could only go for two days and one night—his mother needed his help with the little girls, and he was still working with his dad to turn the store into a church, but two days worked for me too. My dad had half a dozen projects around the house that he wanted me to do.

The Cascade Mountains are close to Seattle. We got an early start so we reached Kachess Lake in the morning. As we drove through the campground, I saw girls our age on the lake roaring about on Jet Skis. It would have been fine by me to skip the backpacking and instead spend the next couple of days hanging out on the beach.

If Levi noticed the girls, he didn't say anything. I drove past the lake and through the campground to the trailhead. While he filled out the paperwork and dropped the fee into the fee box, I unloaded the trunk.

I figured we'd just sling our packs over our shoulders and start walking, but Levi had a long checklist — compass, food, water, emergency blankets, matches. It wasn't enough to tell Levi I had the item; I had to hold it up so that he could see it. The one thing I thought important — a cell phone — he didn't own.

About halfway through, I got frustrated. "We're only going out for one night, Levi. It's no big deal if we don't have something. We'll survive."

"Only a fool goes into the mountains unprepared," he said.

That shut me up.

At last we started up the trail. For the first mile, we saw kids with their parents out on day hikes. The second mile there were fewer people, mainly guys with their girlfriends. We'd smile and they'd smile, and for the first time in my life I wondered if somebody might think I was gay — a thought I didn't like at all. Three miles out we saw backpackers, and now guys with their buddies outnumbered guys out with their girlfriends.

Parts of the trail were steep. One spot was more than a little scary; a misstep and it was a long fall into a ravine — instant death.

The backpack straps dug into my shoulders, but Levi didn't complain, so I kept my mouth shut.

As we hiked higher up into the mountains, I'd point to something and say: "That looks cool," and then Levi would tell me all about it. Trees, birds, mushrooms, and insects — he knew about everything. He spotted cougar poop and explained how he could tell it wasn't bear poop, not that I really wanted to know. "You can feel God here," he said. "You can feel his perfect goodness."

At Thorp Lake, we searched for a place to set up camp. I saw a dozen spots that looked fine, but Levi found something wrong with each one. He was carrying the tent, so I trudged along, quiet, waiting.

Finally he found an area that satisfied him: high ground, flat land, and layers of composting leaves to make the earth softer. He insisted that we set up the tent perfectly, stretching out the ropes and pounding in the pegs until our campsite looked like a magazine ad.

We started a fire and roasted hot dogs; I wolfed down three along with a half pound of dried apricots. I'd packed the fixings for s'mores. We made some, ate them, made some more, and ate them too. As we ate, Levi told me about watersheds and how they clean the earth. I found myself yawning just as the first stars were coming out. I called it a night and headed into the tent. I didn't think I'd sleep well, but I didn't stir when Levi came into the tent.

In the middle of the night, I had to pee. I unzipped the sleeping bag and the front of the tent, and then staggered outside. The fire had gone completely out, but it wasn't dark. I looked up and understood why.

Thousands of stars were shining down on me — way more stars than I'd ever seen on the clearest night in either Redwood City or Seattle. I could actually see the Milky Way wind its way across the heavens. I stared up at the stars until the cold forced me back to the tent and into my sleeping bag.

The next morning I was sore, especially the back of my thighs. As we ate dried fruit and hot oatmeal for breakfast, Levi said he would have liked to keep walking deeper and deeper into the woods. I pretended to agree, but the Milky Way had been enough for one trip.

As we hiked down, the sky clouded over. Rain hadn't been predicted, but that didn't stop the clouds from opening. I had nothing that could stand up against the onslaught, but Levi had packed a rain parka for himself and a spare one for me.

It took far less time to come down the mountain than it had taken to go up. At the trailhead, we loaded our soggy stuff into the Subaru. I made a mental note to clean the trunk before returning the keys to my mother.

As we pulled onto I-90, I suddenly wished I were alone, which probably comes from being an only child. I was afraid Levi would want to talk about . . . about what? I didn't want to hear any more about ferns or mushrooms or beetles. Luckily, he surprised me. "I'd like to sketch, if that's okay."

So he sketched and I drove, U2 playing through the car speakers. Once in a while, I peeked over at his work. He drew birds, trees, and flowers — all the things he'd pointed out to me as we'd hiked. He'd do a bird from the side, then the same bird straight on, from behind, sitting on a branch, flying. The instant he finished one animal or plant, he would turn to something new.

He worked nonstop, filling page after page. They were amazing drawings, but they were slightly crazy, too. Why draw twenty versions of one leaf? Once he started drawing something, he didn't seem to know how to stop.

13

WHEN LEVI AND I RETURNED to Green Lake the next afternoon, the first person we saw was Ryan Hartwell. "Where were you guys?" He seemed almost angry.

When I explained that I'd gotten my mother's car and that we'd gone backpacking, his expression changed. "I love the mountains," he said. "If you ever need somebody to get you up into the backcountry, just ask. I'll go anytime — rain, snow, or shine."

Cash came in then, his big smile and loud voice announcing his return. A couple minutes later, Nick and DeShawn strolled through the door. I hadn't expected many other high school players to show up, but after two weeks of skimpy turnouts, nearly everyone had returned. We had ninety minutes of solid games that day, and then again every day for the following week. When we weren't playing, Hartwell was giving us tips. Everything was so good I wanted it to go on, but when I looked at the calendar one Saturday morning, it was September 3. School was just a few days away.

That afternoon we played our best basketball of the summer. Cash and I hadn't become friends, but we'd become teammates.

We won four in a row before we lost one of those games where nobody can buy a bucket. Even in that game, we played as a unit.

After the last game, we stood at center court, looking at one another and feeling satisfied with what we'd accomplished. Finally Cash, DeShawn, and Nick said they were heading out. They'd reached the door when Hartwell, who'd been watching all afternoon, called them back.

"What's up?" Cash asked.

"To thank you for letting an old guy hang out with you this summer, I'm having a Labor Day party on Monday. I live across the street in the apartment building above Road Runner Sports. Number 212. There's an interior courtyard with a swimming pool. I'll order some pizzas. You can swim or just hang out at the pool with the girls."

DeShawn and Nick looked at Cash. "Sure," Cash said. "Sounds good."

Hartwell turned to Levi and me. "How about you two?"

With the gym closed for Labor Day, I'd have nothing to do on Monday except work for my dad, and I didn't want to do that all day. Besides, Hartwell had done so much for us. "Okay," I said, and it was understood that I was also speaking for Levi.

"Great," Hartwell said. "Monday around two. And you guys had better show. I don't want to be sitting around with three large pizzas and nobody to help me eat them."

14

A T TWO ON MONDAY AFTERNOON, Levi and I were standing in the lobby of the apartment building, staring at the call button next to Ryan Hartwell's name, neither of us eager to push it. We might have slipped away, in spite of our promise, but then Cash, DeShawn, and Nick came in. DeShawn and Nick hung back, but not Cash. "There's his name," he said, pointing. "What are you waiting for? Push the button."

So I did. Immediately Hartwell's voice came through the intercom. "I'll buzz you in." Three minutes later, all five of us were in his apartment.

It was a nice place — brand-new — but without much furniture. In the main room, Hartwell had one sofa, a plasma TV on the wall, a half-filled bookcase, and that was it. Through an open door, I could see a mattress laying on the floor of his bedroom, clothes piled up around it.

"Make yourself at home," he said.

The sliding-glass door to a balcony was open. I stepped outside and looked over the swimming pool. As Hartwell had promised, scattered around it were a bunch of girls in bikinis lying on chaise lounges, cold drinks on little metal tables next to them. What he hadn't mentioned was that nearly all of the girls had a guy lying on a chaise lounge next to them.

The pizza came. We ate as we listened to old Elton John songs on Hartwell's sound system. "You want to go down and swim?" Hartwell asked when about half of the pizza was gone.

I had swim trunks on under my shorts and so did Cash. We waited while the other guys changed in Hartwell's bedroom, and then we all went down to the pool. Most of the chairs and chaise lounges were taken, but I'm not much for lying around anyway. I slipped into the pool; the temperature was in the eighties, so the cool water felt great. But once I was in the water, I wasn't quite sure what to do. All those twenty-somethings around the pool made me feel like a little kid.

The other guys were also subdued. Nobody tried to dunk or splash anybody. For a second I thought that maybe I'd swim laps, but the pool was too small for that. I understood why everyone else was sitting around the pool and not swimming in it. You could use the pool to cool off, but that was all it was good for.

After a few minutes of flopping around aimlessly, Cash headed back up to Hartwell's apartment. I looked at a couple of the girls who were sitting on the chairs around the pool. They weren't girls; they were women — eight, ten, twelve years older than me. I decided to go back up too.

I changed back into my shorts in Hartwell's bedroom. When I came into the living room, Cash was sitting on the sofa going through Ryan Hartwell's DVDs.

"These are hot," Cash said to no one as he stuck a DVD into the player. I headed into the kitchen for a slice of pizza. When I came back out, a babe wearing a tiny bikini and chugging beer filled the plasma screen. "Take it off!" Cash yelled at the screen, laughing, and it was clear that that was what she was about to do.

But Hartwell hit the Pause button on the remote. I was certain he was going to hit the Eject button next. Instead, he stood in front of his TV, blocking the screen. "Listen up," he said, sounding like a coach at the beginning of practice. "I'm twenty-five now, but I remember what it was like to be seventeen. Here are my rules. I've got beer in a cooler out on the balcony. Each of you can have two — no more. And if you drove here, you don't leave until one hour after you finish the last beer."

Cash's eyes widened. "You bought beer for us?"

Hartwell nodded. "I bought beer for you. Two each, like I said, but no more. And you can watch whatever movies you want — just don't go telling your moms." He smiled. "What happens in apartment 212 stays in apartment 212. Okay?"

"Yeah, sure," Cash said, speaking for all of us.

"All right, then," Hartwell said, grinning. "Enjoy yourselves."

Cash stood and looked at us. "Beers all around?" he asked as he headed to the balcony. While he was outside, the girl on the TV screen turned her back to the camera, undid her bikini top, and let if fall. "Get back in here, Cash," DeShawn yelled. "You're missing the best part."

Cash came rushing back holding a six-pack of Budweiser. He passed them out. One for each of us. Only Levi wouldn't take his. "I'm going home," he said.

"What?" Cash said in disbelief. "You got babes on the screen, you got a beer in your hand, you got pizza in your mouth — and you're leaving?"

"I'm going home," Levi repeated, and he headed out onto the balcony to get his swimsuit, which was drying in the sun.

I sat frozen, my eyes on the screen. Three girls were sliding into a hot tub. I wanted to stay; I wanted to drink beer and eat pizza and look at beautiful girls. Levi was going, but that didn't mean I had to leave. Then, suddenly, I knew. I stood and handed my unopened beer to Cash.

"I'm leaving, too."

"You two are both nuts," Cash said, disbelief on his face.

"Let them go," DeShawn said. "It means more beer for us."

"No, it doesn't," Hartwell said. "Two each. No more."

I went out to the balcony to grab my wet swimsuit and then hustled to catch up with Levi. Hartwell trailed behind me. "Everything is okay, right?" he said. "You're not going home and telling your parents about any of this?"

I shook my head. "Don't worry. We wouldn't do that."

Levi was opening the door to the stairwell. "Wait for me, Levi," I called to him, but he didn't wait. I turned back to Hartwell. "He's very religious. His father is a minister. If it was up to me, I'd stay, but —"

Hartwell put both his hands on my shoulders and looked me in the eye. "You're being a friend, Jonas. Never apologize for being a friend."

When I got down to the street, Levi was half a block away. I had to run to catch up with him. "You could have stayed," he said when I reached him. His voice was shaky, as if he was near tears.

"I wasn't having that great of a time," I said.

We walked about twenty-five yards in silence.

"'What would Jesus do?'" Levi finally said. "That's what I ask myself when things like that happen. The answer always comes, and then I do what Jesus would do."

I wondered: Was it really that simple? Who knows? Maybe when Jesus was seventeen, he'd have had a beer and watched the babes. I smiled at the thought, but I didn't say anything to Levi. I knew better than to make that kind of joke with him.

PART THREE

1

MY HOUSE WAS MORE THAN a mile from Harding High. There was no school bus, but I wouldn't have taken one anyway. My mom told me that she'd give me a ride if it rained hard, but that most days I'd have to walk.

I'd arranged to stop by Levi's house on the first day. He must have been looking out his window for me, because he came tumbling out of his house when I was still twenty-five yards away. He seemed tense, stopping three times to check his backpack for supplies as we walked along. You'd have thought he was the new student at Harding.

As we neared the school, the sidewalks started filling with kids. Some would see Levi and holler, "Hey, Double D, what's up?" I hated the easy way kids used that nickname. Every single guy who called him that — and it was all guys — was smaller than Levi. I don't know much about the Bible, but I know Christ once threw moneylenders out of the temple. Levi needed to throw some of these "Double D" jokers onto their asses. Do that to a few of them, and the rest would stop.

Once we'd stepped inside the big double doors, Levi and I

separated. The one class we had together was health, which came at the end of the day. As soon as he was gone, I felt an ache in my stomach. During the summer, I'd worried about what Coach Richter expected from me on the basketball court. Once I stepped inside Harding High, it was his academic requirements that came flooding at me.

In my first two classes — English and Algebra II — the teachers passed out a syllabus, warned everyone not to fall behind, and promised that we'd learn a lot if we studied hard. The other kids leaned back in their chairs and rolled their eyes; they'd heard the same lecture for years. I'd heard it too, but I felt as if it were Richter in the front of the classroom, his intense eyes warning me not to blow my chance. Both Mrs. Miller and Mr. Wunderlich had kind smiles. Maybe I'd be okay with them.

Chemistry, my third-period class, wasn't okay. Mr. Butler was an old-school, no-nonsense type, with a receding hairline and a shiny scalp. He wore a brown suit and a skinny brown tie.

Once the bell rang, Butler strode up and down the rows. "I'm not like most teachers. I won't give you a C for breathing. A C in my class means you have an average knowledge of chemistry. If you have a below-average knowledge of chemistry, you can expect a D or an F."

He growled on like that for a while before he sat down behind his desk, which was front and center, and stared out at us. For a long minute, the silence was heavy. Then a thick, short finger was pointed like a gun at my forehead. "Name?"

"Jonas Dolan," I managed.

"Okay, Jonas Dolan, tell me something about the periodic table."

A roaring filled my ears. Every kid in the class was staring at me. What could I say? I didn't know anything about the periodic table.

"Come on, come on," Butler spat the words at me like bullets. "You must know something about the periodic table."

Kids around me laughed, nervous laughs, *Thank God I'm not him* laughs. When I felt like I was about to fall apart, a dark-haired girl looked over at me. She mouthed a word.

"Oxygen," I said. "Oxygen is on the periodic table."

Butler clapped slowly and maliciously. "Brilliant, Jonas Dolan. Absolutely brilliant. Taxpayers will be delighted to know that the money they have coughed up for your education has not been wasted. You've heard of oxygen. Amazing." He turned from me and honed in on Edward Yang, a bright-eyed Asian kid in the first row who knew about uranium, plutonium, and everything else on the periodic table. The praise Butler gave him wasn't sarcastic.

2

I HAD LUNCH AFTER MRS. CLEMENTS'S fourth-period American government class, but instead of going to the cafeteria, I went to see Mrs. Stone, my counselor. When I told her I wanted out of Butler's chemistry class, a smile crept across her face. "You're not the first student who has said that to me."

She spun around in her chair to face her computer. Screens came up and screens went down. After about two minutes she turned back to me. "Keyboarding. Or you could be a library assistant."

"I need a lab science."

"You've already taken biology."

"Doesn't somebody else teach chemistry?"

She raised her eyes. "At Harding chemistry means Mr. Butler."

"What about physics? Could I take physics?"

"Chemistry is a prerequisite." She paused. "Should I switch you to keyboarding?"

I took a deep breath and exhaled. "No, I'll stick with Butler."

She looked surprised. "Okay. But if you decide to switch later, it'll be harder."

I had Spanish fifth period with Mr. Contreras, and as my

classmates struggled to introduce themselves in Spanish, I half considered slipping out of the classroom to phone Coach Richter to tell him I had a crazy man for a chemistry teacher and to plead with him to drop the laboratory-science part of the deal. But the other kid Richter was considering for the scholarship — whoever and wherever he was — that kid wasn't going to drop classes. He was probably going to get straight As.

I was thoroughly depressed as I headed to health. When I stepped into the classroom, I scanned the room, finally spotting Levi way in the back. "Hey," I said, when I closed in on him, "how's your day going?"

He shook his head and frowned. "My classes look tough."

"Teachers always try to scare you on the first day."

The bell rang, and Ms. Fleming, the only one of my teachers who was under thirty, ran through her version of the opening statement. I took no notes, because there was absolutely nothing important said, but Levi filled three pages of binder paper. A couple of times I looked over to see what he could possibly be writing. *Quizzes every few weeks . . . Keep up with new medical developments . . . Healthy life choices are important.*

I wondered if that was why he had trouble passing his classes. Maybe he studied the same way he drew animals and trees, looking at everything from every angle. Maybe he needed to learn what to ignore.

3

ONCE CLASS ENDED, LEVI AND I headed over to the gym for unofficial basketball practices. As we walked down the long hall, I grew more worried about Coach Knecht. "Does Knecht watch these games?" I asked.

Levi shook his head. "That's against the rules. Coach Knecht will stop by only to say hello.

When we turned the final corner leading to the gym, I spotted Cash joking with a tall man wearing a coat and jacket. The man had his back to me, but he stood straight — nothing bent over about him — so I knew he couldn't be Knecht. Cash saw Levi and me and called out, his voice excited. "Double D, Jonas — look who's teaching here."

The man turned around.

It was Ryan Hartwell.

Smiling ear to ear, Hartwell strode toward us, his hand raised so we could high-five him. "Good to see you again, Levi. Good to see you, Jonas. What am I saying? It's great to see you. It's fantastic."

"Are you a teacher here?" I asked.

"Social studies and PE," he answered, his eyes alive.

"Why didn't you tell us in the summer?"

"Because I got hired yesterday."

"It gets better," Cash broke in. "He's our basketball coach too."

"Assistant coach," Hartwell quickly added, looking at Levi. "Mr. Knecht is still your head coach."

Within minutes DeShawn and Nick came up, and Hartwell told his story again. Then he pointed to the locker room. "Get in there and get changed. You guys need work. Remember, I saw how bad you were all summer."

The girls' varsity volleyball team had the main gym, but Coach Knecht had arranged for us to use a side gym so small that there was hardly any space between the out-of-bounds line and the wall. I was the first guy out on the court and immediately started to shoot around. The other guys came onto the floor soon after me. I recognized Brindle, my competition, because he dribbled the ball with the confidence of a point guard. His shooting form was not bad — the guy had obviously gotten a lot of good coaching — but the results were just okay. The same thing was true with his speed and quickness: good, not great.

We'd been on the court about ten minutes when Coach Knecht came in. His back was bent exactly as Levi had described, but he had a strong jaw, a grizzled beard, and hawkish eyes that seemed to look right through you. He said hello to the guys he knew, and then he had us new guys tell him about our basketball backgrounds.

"So you played point guard in California?" he asked when I finished. "Did you start?"

"Yeah, I did."

"'Yes, sir,' would sound better."

My face turned bright red. Knecht let me squirm a little and then continued. "Were you any good?"

"Yes, sir. I was good. I was second-team all-league."

"I meant your team, Jonas. Was your team good?"

Another wave of heat burned through me. "Yes, sir, the team was good."

He looked at Brindle. "Looks like you've got competition, Donny."

Then Knecht turned to another new guy and started over with the questions.

"Here's how it will work," he said, after he'd heard from every player. "You'll have this side gym every day from two thirty to four, and the weight room from four to four thirty. If you can make the sessions, great. If you need the time to study, then study."

Knecht left, and DeShawn sidled over to me. "Sorry I didn't tell you about the 'Yes, sir' stuff." Then he nodded toward Brindle. "Word is he didn't get many minutes on that fancy-ass select team he played for all summer. His parents paid a ton of money for nothing. If you ask me, you're better than he is."

4

CASH CHOSE THE TEAMS THAT day and every day. I don't know why he was the one to do it, but nobody objected. There are people like that — people who run things — and Cash was one of them. He put himself with Brindle, which irked me until I remembered that Brindle had spent the previous season feeding Cash. It would have been pretty cold for Cash to choose me as point guard for his team. I did end up with Levi and DeShawn on my team, so I wasn't stuck with a team of total strangers.

Early in that first game, Brindle got right up into my space, his butt low, slapping his hands on the gym floor to show me he meant business, bumping me whenever he could. It was 50 percent good defense and 50 percent attempted intimidation.

I didn't react to any of the showboat antics; I simply played my game. If he was overly aggressive, reaching in too far, I'd turn on the burners and take him to the hoop. But I did that only when he guarded me closely. A point guard's job is to run the team, and that means getting teammates involved, not getting caught up in one-on-one competition.

Brindle could play, so it wasn't as if we were in a dumb movie where I stole the ball from him all the time and scored at will. I held my own, though. The games went to eleven, just like the games at Green Lake, and my team won more than we lost, despite the fact that Cash was on fire from long range.

It was closing on four — which was when Knecht had told us we had to leave the gym — and I could feel Brindle wearing down. That's when I did make it one-on-one. My best moment came on the last play. Brindle brought the ball into the forecourt, directing traffic. When his dribble got a little high and a bit sloppy, my left hand slapped the ball loose. I pounced on it and then raced upcourt. Brindle was backpedaling, totally out of position. At the free-throw line, I crossed over. I was by him in the blink of an eye, so I didn't see him go down, but when I looked back after making the gimme, he was on his butt, and the guys were laughing.

At precisely four o'clock, the girls on the JV volleyball team took the court. I hated to stop, and I didn't look forward to what came next — the weight room. I've never liked weightlifting, but something Hartwell had said in the summer had stuck. *"If you're strong enough to shoot through a foul, you've got a chance for a three-point play. If the foul stops your shot, the best you're looking at is two free throws."* I forced myself to put in a solid thirty minutes of lifting, working with Levi as my partner.

At four thirty Levi and I picked up our backpacks and duffle bags from the locker room. I was hungry and wanted to get home to eat, but as soon as we stepped into the gym lobby, Hartwell appeared from around a corner. "Can I talk to you two for a minute?"

We followed him into the coaches' office in the back of the main gym. Through the glass, I could see the girls' varsity volleyball team finishing up their practice. Celia Chavez — the girl who'd helped me come up with the word *oxygen* in chemistry class — caught my eye. I gave her a wave, and she waved back.

"Sit," Hartwell said, so Levi and I plopped down in plastic blue chairs. Hartwell positioned himself behind a big oak desk. "I spoke with Cash and those guys earlier," he said, leaning forward. "They're on board; I'm hoping you will be too."

"On board with what?" I asked.

Hartwell tapped his fingertips together and then resumed. "When I gave that party at the end of summer, I hadn't been hired by Harding High. Had I known I'd be hired, I wouldn't have done what I did." He shook his head slowly. "If word ever got out about the beer and those movies, my career would be over before it even started."

"I won't tell anyone," I said.

"Neither will I," Levi put in.

Hartwell gave a sigh of relief. "I was hoping you'd say that." He paused. "One more thing. I'd appreciate it if you didn't mention to Coach Knecht that I worked with you guys at Green Lake. A coach can't run practices in the summer. There was nothing wrong with what I did. I hadn't yet been hired and those weren't really practices — but if Coach Knecht were to find out, he'd feel honor bound to report it. That would trigger an investigation. I'd be cleared, but it would take a long time, and who needs the hassle? I'm not asking you to lie; I'm just asking you not to mention it."

Again I nodded, and Levi did too.

Hartwell's stood and stuck out his hand. "I owe you. If down the road there's anything I can do for you, just ask."

5

A COUPLE OF WEEKS INTO SEPTEMBER, I got an e-mail from Coach Richter asking me how school was going. His question forced me to take a good, hard look at myself. Was I going to meet Monitor College's academic requirements? As I sat staring at my computer screen, I evaluated myself the way I'd evaluate a player on an opposing team.

Richter had said I'd need a 3.0 grade point average this year. The health textbook looked like something for fifth-graders; I'd have a chance for an A in that class. In Spanish, Mr. Contreras mainly talked about Spanish culture and then had us practice conversations. I've got good pronunciation and can roll my *r*'s. A B in Spanish looked like a lock.

Algebra II with Wunderlich was manageable. All the extra work with Mr. Nutting back at Redwood High had paid off. It was early, and the work was review, but I had a good feeling.

My English and American government classes were going to be time eaters because of the reading and the homework. If I wasn't playing basketball all the time, I was pretty sure I could pull a B in both. I *was* playing basketball, though, so making Bs was going to be hard. Still, I had a chance.

That left chemistry with Butler. When Butler wrote chemical equations for us to copy down, he'd pound his chalk into the blackboard (he was probably the last guy in the school to use one), making white pieces fly in all directions. In the lab, he assumed everybody knew grams and liters. On the first quiz, I'd gotten a sixty; on the first lab, a D.

In my reply to Richter, I was honest. I told him the good stuff, the in-between stuff, and — at the very end — I admitted that chemistry would be a battle. Better to let him know the truth than to pretend. The next day I got an e-mail back. "I checked with the admissions office. A C in chemistry will be fine, but Monitor College doesn't accept Ds."

6

HEALTH WAS THE ONLY CLASS I had with Levi, but I often saw him during passing periods and at lunch. Most six six guys strut in the halls. A freshman or sophomore gets in his way, and he'd better get *out* of his way. Levi moved — there's no other word — *gently* through the school. He held doors for freshmen who were fumbling with their backpacks. If somebody dumped his books, he'd stop and help him pick them up. Harding has its guys in wheelchairs, its kids with cerebral palsy, its kids who can't talk right. I avoid them — I know I shouldn't, but I do. Levi went out of his way to prop open a door or move a desk to make a path wider — little things that were big things for those kids.

It didn't seem fair. Here's this guy with a huge heart, always looking for ways to make life better for every single person he meets, and life was so hard for him. Every day in health class, he filled pages of his notebook, drowning himself in details, writing with a dull pencil, and pressing down so hard that the blank pages underneath turned crinkly.

I tried not to look at his quizzes when Ms. Fleming returned them, but it was like coming up on an accident while driving on the freeway—you can't keep from peeking at the crumpled cars. Levi's scores were never higher than seventy and were usually lower. If he was floundering that badly in an easy class like health, what were his other grades like?

I wanted to offer to tutor him, but I was too worried about my own grades. Even with all the hours I spent studying, chemistry still looked like a disaster. One good thing had happened: Butler had made Celia my lab and study partner. We made a good team. She was better than me at understanding the concepts, but I had the better touch in the lab.

7

I WAS TENSE ALL OF THE time, thinking about Monitor College or chemistry or Brindle or Coach Knecht. After dinner I'd study in my room for at least an hour and usually two. If I finished my homework and it wasn't absolutely pouring rain, I'd borrow my mother's car and drive to the Good Shepherd Center, where I'd shoot around by streetlights. It was often windy or drizzly, so I didn't make many shots. Still, dribbling the ball, banking in a few jumpers, sinking a free throw—doing those things soothed me—until the next day when the battle would start over again.

Levi was struggling too. In mid-October he told me he had to quit the after-school basketball workouts. "You can't quit," I said. "We're doing great out there. You know we are. All the things Hartwell taught us are coming together."

"I'm failing my classes, Jonas. I need that time to study."

"There's got to be some other way."

"What way?"

He stared at me, waiting. My mind raced. "Listen. Here's what we'll do. We'll scrimmage after school, just like we usually do, but we'll skip the weightlifting and instead go straight to my house.

That'll save us at least half an hour, maybe more if we walk fast. Once we get there, I'll help you with your homework. Okay?"

He winced. "You don't know how dumb I am."

"You're not dumb, so don't say that. People thought Einstein was dumb and look what he ended up doing. You can pass your classes, Levi. Just let me help you."

So instead of pumping iron in the weight room the next afternoon, we sat side by side at my kitchen table reviewing for a health quiz we were having the next day. Levi laid his insanely long class notes on the table, and I read through them with him, highlighting in yellow the important things.

"How do you know what's important and what isn't?" he asked.

I shrugged. "I don't know; I just do."

I glanced at the clock. Prepping for the health test had taken thirty minutes. On the table was his math book. I'd planned on reading a Ray Bradbury short story before eating dinner. After dinner I had some algebra problems to do. If I didn't cut my time with Levi, I was looking at a really late night.

Levi sensed my tension. "I'll go. You've got your own homework."

"No," I insisted. "Stay another thirty minutes."

We moved to the front room so my mom could make dinner. Levi was taking some sort of simplified math class, and the word problems were killing him. One was about a guy who spent half his money on shoes and then half of what he had left on a shirt and half of what was left after that on socks and at the very end had four dollars in his pocket. I must have explained it to him five times. He finally got it, and just then my mom came out. "Why don't you stay for dinner, Levi? We're having spaghetti; there's plenty."

"No, thank you. We always eat together; our whole family."

"Always?" my mother said, disbelief in her voice. "Your whole family?"

"Always," Levi repeated.

After Levi left, my mom and I sat down to eat. She told me about how much she liked the people at Great Clips. "This move is going to work," she said, "that is, if the rain doesn't get to us."

I thought I was my normal self, but halfway through the meal she put down her fork and stared at me. "What's wrong, Jonas?"

"Nothing's wrong."

"No, something is. Why don't you tell me about it?"

I started with Levi, explaining how important he was to my performance on the basketball team and how badly he was struggling in class. I described his incredible drawings and how he was a walking encyclopedia on birds and plants and animals. "If I don't help him, he'll flunk his classes. He won't play, which means I probably won't play, and I can kiss Monitor College goodbye. But if I do help him, then *my* grades will be shot — especially my chemistry grade — and I have to get at least a C." I frowned. "I don't know what to do."

My mom thought for a long moment. Then she straightened in her chair. "Jonas, have you told your coach any of this?"

I shook my head.

"Go to your coach tomorrow. Tell him exactly what you've told me. I bet he'll find a way to help both Levi and you."

8

THE NEXT AFTERNOON I FINISHED Ms. Fleming's health test in twenty minutes. The test took Levi the full period, though he was smiling afterward. "You were right about what to study," he said, amazement in his voice.

In the games after school that afternoon, Levi rebounded like a demon, filled the lanes on fast breaks, and even slammed down one thunderous dunk that shook the backboard.

Ten minutes before we had to give up the gym, Hartwell stopped in, shouted out some advice, and then headed to his office. When the JV volleyball team took over the court, I told Levi I had to check out a chemistry book from the library.

Once he'd left the gym, I headed straight to the coaches' office. I planned to give Hartwell a short version of what was happening, but Hartwell asked question after question, so I ended up telling him not only about school, but also about Levi's drawings and his knowledge of animals and plants. Then Hartwell asked me what Levi's family was like. I gave him a puzzled look. Why would he want to know about Levi's personal life? "I'm not being nosy," Hartwell explained. "The more I know about him, the more I can help him."

Hartwell was like that — he always had an answer.

I ended up telling him all about Levi's father and mother and sisters, about Arkansas and their religion. Eventually we worked back to the main topic. "He tries to learn everything, so he gets overwhelmed. At least that's how I see it. I'd like to help him, but — "

"But you've got your own classes to study for," Hartwell finished for me.

I nodded. "You know about Monitor College. I can't keep up my grades and help Levi, too." I paused. "I was hoping you could find somebody who could tutor him."

Hartwell leaned back in his chair. "You came to the right person. I do know someone who can tutor Levi."

"Who?"

He smiled. "Me."

Hartwell explained that Harding's principal, Mr. Diaz, required every teacher to mentor a needy student. "Levi will be my project. He'll be helping me while I'm helping him. Once the afternoon scrimmage ends, he can bring his books in here. I'll go over his assignments with him and then give him a ride home. He'll miss weightlifting, but he's already a bull."

"I can still help him with health," I said, relief washing over me.

"All right. You're his health tutor; I'll cover everything else. Together, we'll keep him eligible."

As I stood up to leave, Hartwell also stood. "I'm glad you came in, Jonas," he said, walking me to the door. "This confirms what I've always thought about you."

"What's that?"

"That you're a natural leader. My hunch is that before the season ends, you and Cash will be co-captains of this team."

I gulped. "You've got to be kidding. I'm just hoping I don't spend the entire season on the bench watching Donny Brindle."

He waved that off. "Things have a way of working out. You'll see."

As I walked home, I kept hearing Hartwell's words. *Natural leader and co-captain . . . You'll see.* He sounded so sure. Was he trying to tell me something? My mind ran through different possibilities. Maybe Knecht wasn't the real coach. Maybe Hartwell had been hired to ease Knecht out. Schools do that sometimes with old guys who don't know when it's time to quit.

9

LEVI WAS OKAY WITH TAKING Hartwell's help, so we settled into a new schedule. We'd play basketball with the other varsity guys until the JV girls' volleyball team took over the side gym. Then Levi would go to Hartwell's office for tutoring. When I headed home, I'd see them in the office, shoulder to shoulder, Levi's head over a book, his pencil working across the page. Once in a while, Levi would skip his time with Hartwell and instead come to my house to study health.

One Saturday at noon, I met up with Celia at Zoka, a coffee shop right in the heart of Tangletown, for a study session. Each of us bought a mocha and a pastry, and then we worked through the chemistry book. After an hour and a half, we were both brain-dead. We got a second mocha and sat in the overstuffed chairs in the corner and talked.

Celia told me that she was headed to Central Washington University. "I'll be the first person in my family to go to college," she said.

"That's great. Way to go."

She smiled. "How about you? What are your plans for next year?"

I explained my chance for a Monitor College basketball scholarship. "I submitted my application last week. There's another guy the coach is looking at. I don't know his name or where he plays, but I've got to beat him out. It's a weird kind of competition, being up against somebody whose name you don't even know."

"You'll do fine," she said, and she smiled again.

It was her smile that gave me the idea. I sucked up my courage. "You feel like playing miniature golf or going bowling or something? I've got my mother's car."

She shook her head. "That's nice of you to ask, but I don't think so. Maybe some other time."

"No problem," I said, knowing my face had turned bright red.

Monday when I entered Harding High's lunchroom, Levi wasn't at our regular table. I scanned the room until I spotted him sitting with Coach Hartwell in a back corner. He had a book open and was looking intently as Hartwell pointed at something on the page.

Levi needed all the tutoring Hartwell could give him, but suddenly I felt lost. Cash and DeShawn were sitting with a bunch of black guys — I didn't fit in there. I sort of knew Gokul Gowri, a tennis player whose locker was next to mine, but not well enough to take the seat next to him. Until that moment, I hadn't realized that Levi was my only real friend at Harding.

I went through the food line, paid, and took my tray over to a table where a kid from my algebra class was sitting. He was playing some game on his phone, but he nodded to me as I sat down.

The next day, and every day after that, Levi and Hartwell were together at lunch. I'd look over at them now and again. Most of the time, Levi had his nose in a textbook, and Hartwell had a pencil in his hand. But sometimes they'd just be talking, their faces intense, each listening closely to what the other said. A stranger looking at them then would have thought that they were best friends.

Halloween rolled around. Both my parents were working, so I passed out the candy. As I dropped mini Snickers bars into little kids' bags, I thought about Redwood City. If I'd been there, I'd have probably gone with Mark to the Haunted House on Middlefield Road and then afterward to the free rock concert out by Pete's Harbor. One thing was certain: I wouldn't have been sitting home alone.

10

I HAD A MAJOR CHEMISTRY TEST two days after Halloween. If I could manage a C+ or B−, my overall grade would be C. If I flunked it . . . I didn't even want to think about what that would mean.

I studied a couple of hours on Wednesday night, and then I got up early on Thursday morning to head to school for one final hour of review. The library was open and empty. I laid my notes on a table and stared at them. I'd taken too many notes — pages and pages. What should I study and what should I ignore? I suddenly understood how overwhelming everything must have felt to Levi.

I plunged in, trying to learn as much as I could, which is why I didn't notice Hartwell until I heard his voice. "Looks pretty impressive," he said, and I jumped. He raised his hands. "Sorry, Jonas, I didn't mean to scare you."

He sat in the chair next to me and flipped through my notes. "Chemistry. That's harder than ninety percent of the classes you'll take in college. How's Butler as a teacher?"

I explained, choosing my words carefully. For all I knew, Hartwell and Butler were friends, though it seemed unlikely.

Hartwell nodded in sympathy. "My high school physics teacher was like that. They make your life miserable." He paused. "Could you just drop the class?"

"No. The coach at Monitor College says I need a C in a lab science class or I can't get in."

"Are you getting a C?"

"Not yet."

"Do you have a back-up plan? Did you get feelers from any school other than Monitor?"

I shook my head. "No. Monitor was the only school that called. If I don't get in there . . ." My voice trailed off.

Hartwell thought for a moment, then stood quickly. "Follow me."

I closed my notebook, stood, and then trailed behind him as he went down a long hallway and into a small room way in the back. In it were a couple of tables with staplers, sticky notes, and paper clips spread out on top. In a corner on a small desk sat an ancient iMac computer.

"What's this place?" I asked.

"It used to be a teachers' workroom, but when the school was remodeled, they put in a new workroom by the main office. This room has been forgotten. I stumbled upon it by accident."

"So why are we here?"

"I want to show you something."

He sat down, switched on the iMac, and motioned for me to pull up a chair. The computer took forever to load, but once it did, the screen filled with folder icons, each with a different teacher's name on it. Hartwell slid the mouse to me. "Double-click on Butler's."

"Me?"

"Yeah. Do it."

I took the mouse and double-clicked. Again it took forever, but at last the folder opened. Inside were a bunch of other folders. Hartwell reached over and pointed to one entitled CURRENT YEAR.

"Try it."

"Won't there be a password?"

"Find out."

I double-clicked.

Again it opened.

Butler didn't have it protected.

My heart raced. On the screen was a file labeled CHEMISTRY. I double-clicked and a long list of files, organized month by month, appeared. Everything was there. The lab assignments, the quizzes, the tests, the answer keys.

Everything.

I looked at Hartwell.

He wagged his index finger, silencing me before I could get out one word. "Jonas, I don't condone cheating, but a bad teacher like Butler — he's the real cheater. He's cheating you out of your chance for a college education."

The room seemed unnaturally quiet. Ten seconds passed. Ten more. At last Hartwell patted me on the shoulder. "I'm going to leave now. If you want, you can e-mail those files to yourself. If you don't want to do that, then close up the computer and forget I ever showed this room to you." He paused. "Take as long as you want to decide. Like I said, this place is never used by anyone. You can find your way back, right?"

I nodded.

With that, he stood and walked out.

Once Hartwell left, my eyes went back to the screen. I'd cheated some in middle school by looking at other kids' papers during tests, but I hadn't cheated since then. Still, what Hartwell said made sense in a way. I was willing to learn, but Butler cared only about smart kids like Edward Yang. Maybe he was cheating me.

I opened up my e-mail account, selected all the quizzes and tests, attached them to an e-mail to myself, hit Send, and then logged out of my e-mail account. Next I double-checked to make certain that I'd left Butler's folder exactly the way I'd found it. When I was satisfied I'd left no trace, I shut the computer down. The whole process took only a couple of minutes, but on that ancient computer, it seemed to take hours. When I returned to the main room of the library, Hartwell was nowhere to be seen.

There was a bank of computers in the back of the library looking out over the practice football field. I sat down in front of the one that was farthest from the librarian's desk, opened my e-mail account, and clicked on the Butler's file labeled TEST — NOVEMBER. There they were: all the questions and all the answers. I took a deep breath. Then, for thirty minutes, I pored over the material. I didn't get it down cold, not by a long shot, but I got enough.

Butler passed the tests back two days later; I had an eighty-six. When Celia saw my grade, her eyes opened wide. "Way to go!" she mouthed.

"Pure luck," I mouthed back, making myself both a liar and a cheater.

11

THE LAST HARDING HAWKS FOOTBALL game was on a Saturday night in the middle of November. I hadn't attended a single game, partly because I'd been studying so much and partly because it would feel weird to walk into a stadium by myself. Then, on the Friday before the game, Celia asked me if I was going. "Maybe. I'm not sure. Why?"

"I was hoping you could give me a ride."

My heartbeat quickened. "Sure, I can give you a ride."

"Can you also give my friend Missy a ride? We normally go together, but neither of us can get a car."

"No problem," I said, my short-lived hopes gone.

When I pulled up in front of Celia's small yellow house near the Burke-Gilman trail, she and Missy came out the front door before I even got out of the car. I drove to Memorial Stadium, and we sat together in the student section, but off to the side. Missy's boyfriend was Colton Banks, the kicker. Every time there was a punt or a kickoff, she'd get excited, but nothing else excited anyone. The evening was cold, dark, and windy. Both teams were terrible; the game had no flow. About fifty times I asked myself why I was there.

Harding lost 13–9 on a last-minute touchdown that was set up by a fumble. Their record was 2–7 or 3–6, something awful like that, so no one was surprised or disappointed. We were leaving the stadium when Ashley Lau, one of Celia's volleyball teammates, rushed up. "There's going to be a party over in Laurelhurst. Everybody on the team is going to be there. You've got to come."

Celia looked at me. "Do you want to go to a party?"

"I don't know," I said, hesitation in my voice.

Ashley smiled at me. "Come to the party. You'll have fun."

"I won't know anybody," I admitted.

"You know Celia and Missy," Ashley said, "and now you know me."

Ashley wrote down an address that meant nothing to me, but Missy guided me as I drove past the University of Washington, through tree-lined, dimly lit streets. Finally I pulled up in front of a fancy brick house with a huge lawn in front.

The party was at the home of one of the boyfriends of a girl on the volleyball team. His parents were out of town for the weekend. We followed the music down into a large basement area. The volume was loud, but not so loud as to get the police called. Celia and Missy immediately latched on to a group of friends. They tried to bring me into the conversation, but I couldn't follow much of what they were talking about.

After a few minutes, Celia was dragged off somewhere by one of her volleyball teammates. I milled around until I found a corner with a big-screen television. I plopped down on a sofa and watched the fourth quarter of a Boise State–Hawaii game. Once the football game ended, I switched to *SportsCenter,* growing more depressed with every fantastic play.

Around eleven thirty, two guys showed up with a couple of cases of beer. They immediately cranked up the music, which made me nervous. If I got caught drinking and Knecht heard about it, that would be it for me. Goodbye scholarship. I couldn't let myself get kicked off a basketball team before tryouts had even started, and in a fancy neighborhood like that one, neighbors called the police.

I searched out Celia. She was still talking to a bunch of her friends, but our eyes met just as one of the guys shouted out, "Beer for everyone!"

I didn't want to come across as a loser, but I couldn't risk staying, either. Just as I was about to go over to her, she came over to me. "Do you want to leave?"

"Yeah. Can you get a ride from somebody else?"

"No, I'll go too. Let me find Missy and see what she wants to do. I'll meet you upstairs, okay?"

Missy wanted to stay, but her kicker-boyfriend hadn't shown up, so I was her ride home. She was angry, though, and she sat in the back seat letting us know it. When I dropped her off, she didn't say a word as she got out of the Subaru. She just slammed the door and went into her house.

As we drove the empty streets, Celia told me she was glad we'd left. "I don't want to do anything to mess up next year. If I got caught drinking and the school suspended me . . ." She shook her head.

"You don't have to explain," I said. "It's the same for me."

I pulled up in front of her house. Before she got out of the car, Celia leaned over and kissed me on the cheek — a kiss a sister would give a younger brother. "I'm sorry Missy was such a bitch. You're a good guy, Jonas."

Then she was gone, up the walkway and into her house.

12

THE FIRST DAY OF BASKETBALL tryouts was Monday. My long wait was finally over.

I tried to concentrate during my morning classes, but I kept thinking about tryouts. During lunch I sat next to that same guy from algebra class, and he told some long story about his brother who was in the army. I was glad to be able to listen and not to have to say anything. At my locker after lunch, I joked a little with Gokul and for an instant wished that I played tennis like him or even golf. Everything was clear for those guys. Either you beat the guy or he beats you. Whether I could or couldn't beat Brindle one-on-one wasn't important; how Knecht saw us was what mattered.

I sat next to Levi in health. When the bell sounded ending class, we made our way to the locker room, where we changed before heading onto the court. Levi was relaxed — he had his position on the team cemented — but I was so nervous, my hands were shaking.

Step one was to make the team. As we shot around, I checked out the competition. Twenty guys were trying out for twelve slots. Two guys were tall but had nothing else going for them. Two others were short and slow — what were they thinking? A couple of other guys had stone hands; three others looked out of shape.

We'd been warming up for ten minutes under Hartwell's eye when Coach Knecht appeared, seeming slower and more bent over than ever. His wiry gray hair was uncombed, and he had a gray-black two-day stubble on his face. He looked more like the cook in some old cowboy movie than a basketball coach.

I slipped over to Levi. "Is he sick?"

"I don't know," Levi said, worry in his eyes.

Knecht motioned for us to form a semicircle around him. He seemed tiny standing before us, but his eyes were still bright. "Give it your best, and you won't have any regrets," he said in a shaky voice. He followed that with a few more things that I could barely hear before he nodded toward Hartwell and then slowly moved off to sit on a folding chair set up along the sideline at half-court.

Hartwell had us pin numbers to our shirts, and we got at it. Once I break a sweat, I stop thinking and simply play, but all that afternoon I stayed tight. Who was calling the shots? Hartwell or Knecht? Sometimes I dribble between my legs or behind my back for no reason. Hartwell would understand moves like that, but Knecht would think I was showboating. Same thing with crossing over on a guy or pumping my fist after a good play — both came naturally to me. Hartwell wouldn't care, but Knecht wouldn't like either.

When we finished the basic drills, Hartwell broke us up into mini-teams for three-on-three basketball. Knecht stayed glued to his chair, all the time taking notes on a yellow pad.

I didn't have Levi or Cash or any of the starters on my team.

The guys I did have didn't know my game, and I didn't know theirs. Nothing went terribly wrong, but nothing went right, either. One play was typical of my day. We were on offense, playing right in front of Knecht. A defender was overplaying this Brandon Taylor kid who was on my team. I was sure Brandon would go backdoor on him. I delivered a bounce pass to the exact spot where Brandon should have been, only he hadn't gone backdoor; he'd popped out for a pass. My perfect assist ended up out-of-bounds. Out of the corner of my eye, I saw Knecht write something down on his notepad. What was it? That I'd made a stupid turnover, or that I'd made a great pass?

For the last twenty minutes, we played five-on-five, using the two side courts. Hartwell moved Levi to my team. For the first part of the tryout, I'd been trying so hard to please Knecht that I'd played lousy. During that full-court scrimmage, I was determined to play my game.

The first couple of times up and down the court, both sides were just feeling one another out. Then Levi made a block and hustled to the corner to retrieve the ball. He hit me with a solid outlet pass near half-court. I didn't have numbers for a fast break, but I pushed the ball anyway, looking for an easy transition hoop. Out of the corner of my eye, I spotted Levi flying toward the hoop, about ten feet behind me. I pulled up, waited a beat, and then lobbed the ball up above the rim. Levi soared up, caught it, and jammed it down.

Both my pass and his finish were fantastic, and guys on both teams were wide-eyed. I was grinning and so was Levi — until we heard Knecht's whistle. The old man was up and out of his seat, energetic for the first time all day.

"What are you doing, Levi?" Knecht demanded as he tottered over, his face bright red, onto the court. Levi hung his head as if he were a toddler who'd been caught crayoning a wall. "Just lay the ball off the backboard," Knecht commanded, his voice stronger than it had been all day. "Just lay it off the glass and in. That's all you need to do."

"Yes, sir."

Hartwell caught my eye and then looked at the ceiling.

13

THE NEXT DAY KNECHT TOOK control. As Hartwell stood off to the side, Knecht called out the names of ten players he wanted at center court for a scrimmage. He sent me and the nine other guys over to a side court to shoot around.

I panicked.

The meaning was clear. I was in a battle with nine guys for one of the final two roster spots. If I had a bad practice — or if a couple of the other guys had a great practice — I wouldn't even make my high school team. All hope of a scholarship would be gone.

Hartwell saw the fear in my eyes and came over to me. "You're okay, Jonas," he said, putting his arm around my shoulder and giving me a shake of encouragement. "You're number eleven on Knecht's chart, and he doesn't even have a number twelve. Once you make the team, he'll see how good you are. You'll get your chance."

His words were like the gift of a hunk of bread to a starving man. All that day, and all the subsequent days of the tryout, I played in-your-face defense, blocked out on defensive rebounds, made safe passes, and didn't turn the ball over. Nothing I did was flashy or very fun, but on Friday, when Knecht posted the roster, my name was on it.

In the locker room, the guys who made the team hung around for a while to celebrate. DeShawn wondered aloud whether the team's style of play would change with Hartwell as an assistant. "Maybe he can drag Knecht into the twenty-first century."

"First he'll have to drag him into the twentieth," Cash said.

Everybody laughed — even Brindle — everybody except Levi. "Come on, Double D, it's just a joke," Cash said. "Knecht's not God."

Later, when I thought over what Cash had said, I realized how on the mark he'd been. People like Knecht and like Levi's father — they were gods to Levi. He had them way up on a pedestal. I thought about my own father. He was a good guy, but he made mistakes, and I knew it. I was glad I didn't think of him as a god, and I'm sure he was too.

14

THAT SUNDAY LEVI'S DAD'S CHURCH held its first services. Weeks earlier Levi had asked me to go, and I'd said yes. Now that the day had come, I was edgy. Was his father one of those crazy preachers who yelled about Satan and sin? And what about the people I'd be sitting with? Would they roll around in the aisles?

The church still looked like a store from the outside, but what Levi and his father had done inside was amazing. Levi had mentioned getting wooden pews from a church that had merged with another congregation. I figured the pews would be old and ratty like something from Goodwill, but they'd been sanded and oiled so that they looked both brand-new and a hundred years old at the same time. The same thing was true of the wood floors, which gleamed in the golden light. The plain wooden altar in the front of the church was lit from above by a spotlight so perfectly positioned that the light seemed as if it were coming from heaven.

The church was a thousand times nicer than I thought it would be, and the service was also far different from what I expected. I'd been worried that I'd be surrounded by a bunch of crazy people constantly screaming about Jesus. Instead, the service was dull.

For twenty minutes, different people came up and read passages from the Bible. Then Levi's father talked. There was no mention of hellfire or damnation; most of what he said was about how Hollywood was making American girls and boys chase after sinful dreams. When he said those words, I glanced to where Levi and his family were sitting, looking for Rachel. She was dressed in church clothes, not the skintight, low-cut outfits she wore at school, but she was chewing gum, and as I watched she blew a tiny pink bubble.

About ten times I thought the sermon was over, but Levi's dad kept talking. The hard seat got harder; my back started to hurt; my nose started to itch; I had to pee. I didn't think he'd ever stop, but finally he led everyone in an Our Father and it was over.

I wanted to leave, but before I left, I searched out Levi. "You did a fantastic job," I said, gesturing to the whole church. "This place is amazing."

He was smiling. I was about to leave when I felt a hand on my shoulder. I turned around, and there stood Ryan Hartwell. Hartwell must have come in after I had because I hadn't seen him during the service. I fidgeted as Hartwell said the same things I'd said, and Levi's smile grew even broader. It was clear that Hartwell was going to hang around for a while, so I slapped Levi on the back, told him how great the church was one more time, and then beat it out of there.

15

AT PRACTICE ON MONDAY, COACH Knecht looked better — at least from a distance. He'd shaved and was wearing a coat and tie. Still, if you got close to him, you could see gray stubble on his chin that he'd missed, and he had a long red gash on his neck where he must have come close to cutting his own throat while shaving.

Once the whole team had taken the court, Knecht talked about the importance of hard work and then sat off to the side while Hartwell ran the drills. Anybody walking into the gym that day would have assumed that Hartwell was the head coach, but the guys on the court knew the playbook was 100 percent Knecht.

Every offensive set started with four players outside the three-point arc. The point guard was positioned at the top of the key. From that basic set, we ran a weave: pass and cut, pass and cut, pass and cut.

If a defender lost focus, then the offensive player was supposed to make a backdoor move to the bucket. The guy with the ball would hit the cutter with a simple bounce pass for an easy lay-up. If the defense stayed alert, then it was up to someone — usually Cash — to knock down a three-ball before the shot clock ran out.

All week Knecht had us practice that basic set over and over. It was boring for us, so it had to be even more boring for Hartwell. He stood on the court, whistle in his mouth, taking instructions from Knecht. I could feel him chafing under Knecht's tight control.

The dustup happened on Thursday. I was point guard on the second team, and my defensive assignment was to guard Brindle. Early on I anticipated a pass and tipped the ball free from Brindle. It wasn't a clean steal, so Brindle was able to get back on defense, but I pushed the ball up-court anyway. Brindle set his feet in the paint, hoping to lure me into a charging foul. I didn't bite. Instead, I drifted to his left and banked in a ten-foot jumper.

The ball was barely through the net when Knecht's whistle sounded. I hoped he'd praise me both for scoring and for avoiding the foul. Instead he wobbled onto the court to let me have it. "If you don't have a lay-up on the fast break, pull the ball out and set up the offense," he growled. "How many times do I have to say it?"

Hartwell came to my defense. "That was a good shot, Coach. Ten feet. Uncontested. A clean look. That's a shot you have to take."

Knecht's eyes flashed. "I'm the coach of this team," he snapped. His eyes came back to me. "If you don't have a lay-up, pull the ball out. Got it?"

"Yes, sir," I said.

Then he turned to Hartwell. "Got it?"

At first Hartwell didn't answer. The two stared at each other. "I got it," Hartwell said at last, and only then did Knecht make his way back to his chair along the sideline.

⊕ ⊕ ⊕

We practiced right up to Thanksgiving break, but when Wednesday's practice ended, Knecht told us to take the rest of the week off. "Family first," he said. The time off was okay with me; I'd run Knecht's weave so many times, I think I could have done it in my sleep.

Thanksgiving wasn't much different from any other night. There'd been some talk of going to Uncle Frank's, but that had fallen through, which was okay with me. The Blue Jay restaurant was open, so my dad was working. I sat across from my mom and ate a turkey leg, some mashed potatoes, and a slice of pumpkin pie. After dinner I went to my room and played video games. I thought about calling Levi and seeing if he wanted to head over to the Good Shepherd Center to shoot some hoops by streetlight, but I knew he'd be at the dinner table with his whole family.

PART FOUR

1

THE SEASON OPENER WAS ON November 30 at home against Juanita High. My mom would be in the stands, but for the first time ever, my dad wouldn't be at my opening game. When I told Levi, he stuck his hands in his pockets and frowned. "My dad has never seen me play."

"Why not?" I asked.

"He says sports games are for children, not for adults."

"What about your mom? Does she come to your games?"

"My mom doesn't understand basketball. Besides, she's got the girls."

The tension before an opening game is about the same as before a championship game. As we suited up in the locker room, everyone was jumpy, laughing too hard at jokes that weren't very funny. Once we were in uniform, Knecht called us together for a moment of silent prayer. Levi closed his eyes and prayed, and Brindle also had his head bowed. Most of the guys looked at one another, uncomfortable.

Once the prayer ended, Cash, as team captain, led us onto the court. Cheers rained down on us from the stands, the adrenaline kicked in, and I felt a familiar tingle up and down my spine.

I could almost believe I was back at Redwood High playing for Coach Russell.

Almost, but not quite. As game time drew nearer, the starters — including Brindle — peeled off their warm-up clothes while the rest of us stayed in our sweats. I felt my spirits start to sink, so I forced myself to stay positive. A lot can happen in a basketball game. Brindle could twist an ankle, commit a bunch of fouls, or turn the ball over and get yanked. Or I could sub into the game to give Brindle a breather, hit a couple of jumpers, and force Knecht to keep me in. "You'll get some minutes," Hartwell had promised me. "Play well and you'll earn more."

The horn sounded and the season was under way. I took my seat on the bench and watched anxiously. Three minutes into the game, Brindle committed his second turnover. I peeked down at Knecht, but the old man had his eyes fixed on the court. Finally, with two minutes left in the first quarter, he pointed to me. "You, get in there for Donny." I reported at the scorer's table and then knelt down, waiting for the next dead ball. With just over a minute left, the ref finally called a foul, stopping play.

A minute to do something.

I did something all right. I drove past the guy guarding me and tossed up a wild shot that didn't even hit the rim. After that stupid shot, I hustled back on defense, staying in front of Juanita's point guard, not allowing him to penetrate. He passed off to a forward who missed from fifteen feet. Levi cleared the boards and hit me with the outlet pass. I wanted to fast break, but from the sideline I heard Knecht: "Slow it down, kid. Set up the offense." So I did. We ran twenty seconds off the clock before Cash hit a jumper to tie the score. Ten seconds later the quarter ended, and at the beginning of the second quarter, Brindle was back on the court, and I was back on the bench.

I didn't get another call from Knecht until the last minute of the second quarter. This time, I didn't make any mistakes, but I didn't *do* anything, either. When the half ended, Knecht patted me on the back. "That's what I'm looking for, kid. No mistakes." His words were like a punch in the gut. Was that all he thought I could do? Did he even know my name?

The score stayed tight throughout the second half. That's how games usually are when a team runs a slow-it-down offense. You don't put up many shots, but neither does the other team. I didn't play in the third quarter, but I got a couple of minutes to start the fourth. Once again, I was like a cardboard cutout of a player; I took up space, ate up time, and did nothing more.

Watching the final minutes of the game while stuck on the bench tore me up. I saw three fast-break opportunities that were wasted. I kept looking at Knecht, but he never even glanced my way. I did catch Hartwell's eye a couple of times. Both times he grimaced and then shook his head.

With thirty seconds left in the game, we had the ball, trailing by a single point. Brindle ran Knecht's offense: pass and cut, pass and cut. With five seconds on the clock, Cash broke backdoor and — for a split second — was wide open. Brindle made the pass, but the ball was inches too far. The ball slipped through Cash's fingertips and out-of-bounds, and that was that.

After the game, the guys dressed and filtered out. I was sitting on a bench in front of my locker, still only half dressed, when Hartwell came over to me and gave my shoulder a squeeze. "Hang in there, Jonas."

2

'M NO QUITTER. I WANTED that scholarship, and I needed playing time to get it. That night I lay in bed, staring at the shadows dancing across the ceiling, trying to figure out how to make Knecht give me those minutes. There was only one sure way: Knecht had to see that I could make Levi into an all-star and that Levi could turn the team into a statewide force.

How to make him see it, though? With any other coach, I could have hit Levi during practice with some backdoor lobs ending in thunder jams. But Knecht wouldn't be impressed by powerful dunks — he'd be angry.

Still, there was a version of that play that Knecht would like. I pictured it in my mind. Levi would cut to the basket; I'd feed him a high lob. Instead of dunking, he'd kiss a soft shot off the glass and through the twine. Knecht would rise up out of his folding chair. "That's basketball," he'd shout. If Levi and I could pull off that play in practice, Knecht would have to give me more minutes in the game.

As we were shooting around that afternoon, I drew Levi aside and explained what I wanted to try. "At least once," I said, "and hopefully a couple of times."

"What if I'm not open?"

"I'll put the ball above the rim where only you can get it, just like we practiced at Green Lake with Hartwell. You can do it. Just don't dunk it, okay?"

I was eager for the scrimmage to begin, but Knecht was Knecht, which meant we did drill after boring drill. As time passed, my excitement ebbed. If we didn't scrimmage, how could I show Knecht what I had?

I wasn't the only one frustrated. Hartwell was using Nick and DeShawn to explain defensive rotations when Knecht stopped him with a tweet on his whistle. "Forget about rotating," Knecht snapped, getting up from his chair and heading onto the court. "They need to work on man-to-man defense, straight up."

Hartwell squeezed the basketball so hard his fingers went white. Then he turned on Coach Knecht. "Coach, you wanted the team to work on fundamentals. Rotating to the ball is fundamental."

"Mr. Hartwell, man-to-man is fundamental. The rest of it comes only after the man-to-man has been mastered."

As he was speaking, Knecht had moved toward Hartwell until there was no more than a few feet between them. Hartwell, eight inches taller and seventy pounds heavier, towered over the old man, but it was Hartwell who backed down. "You heard your coach," he said, turning back to us. "Back to work on your man-to-man defense."

Ten minutes before the end of practice, Knecht finally let us scrimmage. Hartwell refereed, with Knecht still sitting in his folding chair along the sideline at center court. Hartwell mixed up first- and second-stringers to make the teams even, and, as usual, he put Levi on my team.

We'd played a few minutes when I caught Levi's eye. He nodded ever so slightly to let me know he was ready. We worked the ball around the perimeter. DeShawn popped out; I faked a pass to him at the exact moment Levi broke to the hoop. I made an absolutely perfect pass. Levi snatched the ball and, in the same motion, softly kissed the lay-up off the glass and through. When he came down, Levi's excited eyes caught mine. We'd pulled it off perfectly. Then Levi's eyes clouded. Something was wrong. But what? I wheeled around to look at Knecht. I'd expected him to be out of his chair, smiling and giving us a fist pump, but the old guy had his head down and was writing notes on his clipboard.

He hadn't been watching.

That day Levi skipped his tutoring session with Hartwell and instead came to my house to study for a health quiz. We didn't talk about what had happened at practice. What was there to say? Levi spread out his stack of notes on my dining room table, and I helped him whittle them down. When we finished, I asked how Hartwell was as a tutor.

Levi sat straight up. "He knows everything, Jonas. He's the smartest person I've ever met." He paused. "He comes to my father's services now. Every Sunday for the last three weeks he's been there. You're surprised, aren't you? That first time, I figured he was being polite. But it's more than that. Coach Hartwell is looking for God, and when you look for God, God finds you."

3

THE NEXT TEN DAYS WERE one long nightmare. We played three games and won two, but for me they were all losses. Knecht used me strictly as a role player, someone to give Brindle a chance to catch his breath. If I was lucky, I'd get six minutes of playing time over the course of an entire game. Once I played only three minutes, all in the first half. Coach Richter at Monitor College had our schedule. After every game, he'd shoot me an e-mail. *What was the final score? How many assists did I have? Turnovers? Points? Rebounds?*

What did I send him? After four games, these were my grand totals for the season: Six points. Three assists. Two rebounds. Two turnovers. I'd had better numbers by halftime of games at Redwood High. The other kid Richter was considering had to be doing more.

Right in the middle of that stretch, Hartwell pulled me aside in the hallway of school. "Jonas, if you need to talk, I'm ready to listen. You could come see me during my planning period or after school. If you want, you could come to my apartment and watch a movie or study there. Just don't hold it all inside."

"Thanks, Coach," I said, but I did hold it all inside. What else could I do? There was nothing Hartwell could do for me. If I complained to my parents, it would make them feel guilty about the move to Seattle. And I couldn't say anything to Levi. As far as he was concerned, Coach Knecht was just a little bit below God.

On the Saturday morning after our fourth game, Celia and I had arranged to meet at Zoka to study for a chemistry test. Having Butler's files had changed everything for me. I didn't get As on my chemistry tests — that would have been too suspicious. But I was getting Bs, and the class wasn't sucking up every spare minute of my life.

I didn't want to waste time, so for each section I told Celia exactly what to study and what to skip. We'd been studying for about twenty minutes when she pointed to a passage on denatured alcohol. "How come you're so sure we don't need to know this? I think it's important."

For an instant I was rattled, but then a lie came to me. "I looked at study guides on the Internet."

"But Butler might be different."

"He won't be," I insisted. "He hasn't been different yet."

She eyed me suspiciously. "So you've been looking at study guides all along?"

I felt my face redden. "Not all along. Only for the last few quizzes."

She stared at me for a moment longer, but then her eyes returned to the text.

We studied for another hour. All that time, she seemed to feel my deception in the air around her. When we finally called it good, she stood and gave me a tired smile. "See you at school, and thanks." I nodded and then she was gone. I headed home a few minutes later, my head pounding.

4

'D BEEN HEARING ABOUT THE Garfield Bulldogs, our next opponent, all season long. Garfield was undefeated, which was nothing new for them. Year after year, Garfield has won the KingCo District title. Most years they either take the state title or come close. As I watched Garfield go through their pregame drills, I could see that their quickness was a notch above any other team we'd faced.

Just before tip-off, a voice from the stands called out my name. I looked up and saw my dad waving to me. My mouth dropped open — it was the first game he'd attended all year. He must have heard from someone at work that Garfield basketball was special.

For a second I was excited, but then my gut rolled over. At home, I'd pretended I was getting decent playing time. Now he'd learn the truth. When the opening horn sounded, I sank into myself, pulled a towel over my head, and watched Brindle run the team.

Knecht's game plan was to frustrate Garfield by slowing everything down. I'll give him credit — all through the first quarter, his strategy worked. Our pass-and-cut offense forced the Garfield guys to use their energy playing defense. When they finally did get the ball, they raced down the court and fired up quick shots. Sometimes the shot went down; more often the ball clanged off the rim. When that happened, Levi would clear the rebound, pass the ball to Brindle, and Brindle would walk the ball up the court, taking his sweet time to set the offense, and then run the pass and cut, pass and cut, keeping Garfield out of sync. Their fans began booing us. "Play basketball!" a guy behind us kept shouting. I looked down the bench and could see the hint of a smile on Knecht's wrinkled lips.

With one minute left in the first quarter, I stepped onto the court for the first time. I ran the team as if I were Brindle, taking time off the clock, not forcing anything. When the horn sounded ending the quarter, we had played perfect *Knecht* basketball, but our lead was only 10–7.

In the huddle, Knecht was excited. "Eight minutes down, twenty-four to go," he rasped. "We keep playing like this and we'll beat these guys."

Knecht kept me on the court for the start of the second quarter. Twice I thought I had Levi on a lob pass for a lay-up, but I didn't risk it. Instead, I protected the ball as if it were a newborn baby.

Garfield had tightened up their defense on Cash, figuring he was our only offensive weapon. On our first possession, they double-teamed him as soon as he touched the ball. He immediately kicked the ball back to me. I was wide open for a three-pointer. I should have fired it up without thinking, but I was thinking — *Miss this and you're out of the game* — and so I missed, badly. A Garfield guy pounced on the rebound, and they were off on a fast break that ended with a rim-rattling dunk. The crowd roared; Knecht called time-out; and my butt was back on the bench.

The dunk gave Garfield momentum. On our next possession, they trapped Cash along the baseline, forcing a turnover. Again they pushed the ball, except this time Levi was back to defend. The Garfield guard veered off, and then passed to a shooter behind the three-point line. It was exactly the kind of shot Knecht wouldn't let us take, and when it ripped through the net, Garfield had its first lead of the game.

I thought that once Garfield took the lead, they'd swamp us. But Levi kept us in the game by fighting for every rebound and scoring the few points we managed by muscling up offensive rebounds. Still, he couldn't beat Garfield by himself, and at halftime we were down five.

In the locker room Knecht was more animated than I'd ever seen him. "We have to play our game," he urged, beads of sweat forming on his forehead. "Discipline, ball movement — do the little things and you'll win." His voice was hoarse, and his face was a reddish purple.

Guys picked up on his intensity, and in the third quarter, we twice closed the lead to three, but both times a Garfield player hit a three-pointer in transition to push the lead out to six. Then, just before the end of the third quarter, Brindle made two silly turnovers that led to easy lay-ups, kicking Garfield's lead to ten at the close of the third quarter.

During the break between quarters, Knecht growled for me to check-in for Brindle. I hustled to the scorer's table, reported to the guy there, and turned around just in time to see Knecht crumple like a rag doll. Levi caught him on his way down and managed to ease him onto the bleacher seat. There was a collective gasp from the crowd, and then the gym went silent.

A black guy about my dad's age came flying down from the Garfield side. "I'm a doctor! I'm a doctor!" he shouted, and people cleared out for him.

The gym stayed hushed as the doctor bent over Knecht. Knecht looked glassy-eyed, but then he slowly came out of it. "I'm fine," he whispered. "It's just too damn hot in here."

Knecht tried to stand, but the doctor put his hand on Knecht's shoulder, forcing him to stay seated. "Rest a moment, Coach. Then we'll go to the locker room. Once you catch your breath, you can come back out."

Knecht nodded, took a few deep breaths, and then rose to his feet. The doctor tried to help him to the locker room, but Knecht shook free. Everybody stood and clapped, including the Garfield players and coaches, as he left on his own power.

The horn sounded. "One minute," one of the refs said to Hartwell. Hartwell nodded, and then called us to him.

"I want you to run every chance you get." He looked at me. "You hear me, Jonas. Push the ball. It's our only chance."

I looked around at the other guys. They had been staring at Hartwell; now their faces were turned to me.

5

ARFIELD'S COACHES, THINKING THE GAME was salted away, had their second string on the court. On their first possession of the fourth quarter, a guy who looked like an eighth-grader tossed up a wild shot from the corner. Cash snagged the rebound, hit me in stride, and I was off. Because we'd walked the ball up-court the entire game, Garfield wasn't expecting a fast break. DeShawn filled the lane to my right; Levi was streaking toward the hoop on my left. DeShawn had more separation, but I put the ball above the rim on Levi's side. He caught it and slammed it through, something he wouldn't have done if Knecht was on the bench. The backboard rocked, and the Garfield players looked stunned.

On Garfield's next possession, Nick tipped a pass loose and I pounced on it. Again I raced the ball up-court, this time faking to Levi and taking it to the rack myself. I felt the contact, heard the whistle, but still had enough strength to kiss the ball off the glass. It hung on the rim for an instant before dropping through. After I made the free throw, Garfield's ten-point lead had been slashed in half.

Garfield's coach called time-out so that he could bring back his starters, but their heads weren't entirely in the game. I had to keep our energy high, keep the momentum on our side, and not let anyone lose control. One bad pass, one stupid foul, one forced shot, and Garfield would come roaring back. That's how good they were.

For the next few minutes, we played perfect basketball. Nick got a lay-up on a perfectly threaded bounce pass. Levi hit a bank shot after I'd penetrated and then passed the ball out. Cash hit two three-pointers from the corner — the second one tying the game with three minutes left.

Garfield's coach called another time-out, and then another, but we were an express train going full speed. Levi brought down a dunk on an offensive rebound to give us our first lead; DeShawn made a steal and a lay-up at the end to seal the deal. When 00:00 showed on the scoreboard, guys exploded off the bench; Hartwell leaped into the air, and for a minute we jumped around at center court, high-fiving and chest bumping one another. Then we realized we were being jerks, and we lined up and shook the Garfield players' hands.

Once I'd acknowledged every Garfield player, I looked for my dad. He was pumping his fist and shouting, "Great game, Jonas! Great game!"

I gave him a thumbs-up before Hartwell grabbed me by the shoulders and shook me, a huge smile on his face. "That's how to play basketball," he shouted.

I don't know about the other guys, but I'd completely forgotten Knecht. Once I did remember him, I felt guilty. What if he was really sick? Then I spotted him standing at the locker room door, pale but taking everything in.

The locker room was a wild scene. We were energized by the win, amazed at what we'd pulled off. In the middle of it all, Hartwell slipped me a piece of paper. "It's the stat sheet. You've finally got some numbers you can be proud to send to your coach at Monitor College."

6

I FIGURED KNECHT WOULD BE OUT for at least a week, but at the next practice he was sitting in his regular chair. He looked weaker, though he'd never looked strong. After we'd loosened up, Knecht called us to him. "I want you to know that I'm doing fine. Dehydration. Nothing else. That Garfield gym was hot, and I didn't drink enough water. I appreciate the way you played. That win meant a lot to me."

It was hard to know how to respond. Knecht believed we'd dug down deep and won the game *for* him. No one would ever say it, but we'd won *in spite of* him.

Practice began in earnest, and it was as if nothing had changed. Hartwell supervised the drills, but if Knecht saw something he didn't like, he blew his whistle and tottered onto the court, pointing his finger and jawing on about what we'd done wrong. I felt deflated. My fourth-quarter heroics didn't matter; Knecht's return had put me back on the bench.

I assumed Brindle was happy to have Knecht back, but before we took the court for Thursday night's game, he approached me in the locker room. "You should be starting, not me. You deserve to start after the way you played against Garfield."

I was so startled that for a moment I didn't answer. "Coach Knecht wasn't on the bench, Donny," I said, finally. "He doesn't know."

Brindle waved that off. "He must have seen the stat sheet. He has to know how well you played. And they know too." He nodded toward the other guys.

I looked around the locker room . . . at Levi, Cash, DeShawn, Nick. They were quick and athletic, all of them. The running game fit them. I fit them. With me directing an up-tempo, fast-break style of play, there was no telling how far we could go. Only I wouldn't get a chance to play the point, and the team wouldn't get a chance to play up-tempo. I looked back to Brindle. "It's not your fault."

We played two games that week. Coach Knecht sipped water throughout both of them, and he kept a wet towel nearby to wipe his face. When he stood, he rose slowly, never jumping to his feet, and he didn't scream at all.

We beat Ballard High, 36–30, on Tuesday night in what had to be the most boring game in high school basketball history. Two nights later we had an away game against Franklin High. Knecht threw me my usual crumbs — a couple of minutes at the end of the first and second quarters. By the beginning of the fourth quarter, we were down eleven, and Hartwell turned to Knecht. "Jonas could push the tempo, change things up. It worked against Garfield."

Hartwell's tone had been mild, but Knecht stiffened. "We're not playing helter-skelter, not as long as I'm coach. We'll win or lose playing Harding Hawks basketball."

Lose is what we did.

In the locker room afterward, Knecht told us we would have the first week of Christmas break off. "Rest, relax, do things with your family. Clear your minds. After Christmas we'll get back to work."

7

ON THE FRIDAY BEFORE THE break, there was an assembly during sixth period. The band played, some academic awards were passed out, and then Mr. Diaz, the principal, lectured us about drinking and driving over the holidays. "Bad things can happen to good people," he said.

After the assembly, Levi and I had started across the parking lot heading toward home when we heard Hartwell's voice. "Levi, can I talk to you for a second?" Hartwell was standing by the double doors, motioning for Levi. Levi walked back; they talked for a while, and then Levi returned.

"What did he want?" I asked.

"He was setting up tutoring times over the break."

"I didn't think the school was even open."

"We'll meet at the public library, or I'll go to his apartment. I don't want to lose ground." His voice lowered. "Have you noticed?"

"Noticed what?" I asked.

"Nobody calls me 'Double D' anymore. Not even Cash. That's because of Mr. Hartwell and you."

I was about to say something like *You're the one who did the work,* but it sounded too much like teacher talk, so I stayed silent.

As we walked toward Tangletown, we talked over what we'd do during the time off. He had doors to varnish at his father's church, tutoring sessions with Hartwell, and his usual time with his sisters.

"I've got nothing going," I said. "So if you feel like shooting around, give me a call."

After that neither of us said much for five or six blocks. When we reached Levi's house, he turned and faced me. "I'm sorry this season isn't working out for you. I know sitting on the bench must be eating you up."

It felt like a dagger, but I didn't let him know. "There are lots of games left to play. Things could still break my way."

He nodded. "You probably think this is stupid, but I pray for you."

That startled me. "You pray for me?"

Levi nodded. "Not just you. There are lots of people I pray for, but you're one of them."

His voice was so honest; his face was so honest; every single thing about him was so honest that for a split second my throat tightened. Then I made myself smile. "I'll take help from any-where."

We bumped knuckles, and Levi opened the door to his beaten-down home. As soon as he did, one of his little sisters — I think it was Maddie — started squealing his name. I looked back to see him holding her above his head while she kicked with delight.

A couple minutes later, I opened my own front door and stepped into an empty house. I microwaved a pizza for dinner and ate it while watching a Cal-Wisconsin basketball game I'd recorded the night before. My mom came home around seven thirty, and we talked a little. She knew I wasn't having a good season and so did my dad, though neither said anything. My name had sometimes been in the headlines of the *Redwood City Tribune*. In Seattle, with the exception of the Garfield game, my name wasn't even making the newspaper. I didn't bring up basketball, and she didn't, either. Instead, we discussed vacation. "If you don't have practices, what are you going to do with yourself?" she asked.

"I'll be okay," I said. "There's stuff I can do."

After that she went down into the basement to do laundry, and I headed to my room, where I watched *The Fast and the Furious* on my laptop. It was a nonstop action film, but before it had ended, I somehow managed to fall asleep.

8

THE NEXT DAY MY DAD knocked on my door around nine. I was playing a video game, and I quickly shut it down. "You want to earn some money this week?" he asked as he stepped inside.

"Sure."

"Okay. Follow me."

I traipsed behind him down into the basement. He pointed at the insulation in the unfinished ceiling. "See how it's sagging? I want you to shove it back up between the joists. Once it's in nice and tight, nail slats of wood — crisscross style — into the joists. That'll keep the insulation in place. You'll need to hammer a slat every foot or so, or the insulation will sag again. Wear a mask and wear gloves — this stuff is no fun. If you finish here, you can do the crawl space. Same pay as in the summer; you keep track of your hours."

I was glad to be making some money, but it was horrible work. Rats had gotten into the insulation and made nests, so the first thing I did was to bang on the pipes so if any were still around, they'd scamper away. Coming face-to-face with a rat was not something I wanted to experience.

Even though I was working for my dad, the days crawled by. The Blue Jay was busy so my dad was never around; Great Clips was also busy so my mom wasn't home much. Levi was either working with his dad or helping his mom, and when he wasn't doing that, he was studying at Hartwell's apartment.

Neither of my parents had to work on Christmas, so it was sort of an okay day. We ate dinner with Uncle Frank and his wife and their two middle school girls at their waterfront house on Mercer Island. Grandpa and Grandma Dolan had flown up from Arizona. I don't know why, but my dad doesn't get along with his father, so that's why the afternoon was only *sort of* okay. I could feel the tension between them.

Uncle Frank's daughters, Andrea and Alice, showed me around their huge house. There was an entertainment room, an exercise room, a swimming pool, a library, a deck upstairs, a deck downstairs, and about fifty bathrooms and bedrooms. Uncle Frank is a good guy and so is Aunt Clare, and I've got nothing against my cousins, but there was something about all that money that made me happy to get back to my own home in Tangletown. I know my parents were glad to get away, too.

9

WAS RELIEVED TO GET BACK to basketball on Monday. With a Christmas tournament coming up, I expected a long, tough practice, but after only eighty minutes, Knecht blew his whistle and told us we were done for the day. The other guys were also surprised by the short session, but nobody cared much. As a team, we'd given up on being great, and with as much talent as we had, we'd never fall below mediocre. As I was walking off the gym floor, I saw Coach Knecht lean forward in his chair and breathe slowly and deeply, like a man who has just climbed twenty flights of stairs.

This would be his last season; I was certain of it. Still, there was no way he'd turn the team over to Hartwell during the season. He wouldn't quit, not Knecht. I admired him for that. A few times I'd thought about quitting. Why keep torturing myself? I wasn't going to play real minutes, which meant I had no chance to get the scholarship to Monitor College. But quitting isn't in my DNA, just as it wasn't in Knecht's. We had completely different ideas on how basketball should be played, but we had that in common.

Our team was entered in a Christmas tournament down in

Burien beginning on the twenty-seventh: three games in three days at Kennedy High School. We won the first game and then lost the next two. Combined, for the three games, I had ten points, three assists, three rebounds, and zero turnovers in twenty minutes of playing time. I e-mailed the stats to Richter, but I'd stopped writing notes to explain anything. The numbers were what they were.

When the tournament ended, Knecht called us together. "Enjoy New Year's Eve, but don't do anything stupid," he said, sounding just like Mr. Diaz. "You drink and I hear about it, and you're off the team."

10

IN EVERY CLASS AT HARDING High, I had a couple of people I talked to. I joked with Gokul every time I saw him. Still, I wasn't connected with anyone but Levi. The other kids had their groups set; they didn't need or want any new friends. I was just a face.

I didn't expect to get invited to a New Year's Eve party, but I did get an invitation. It wasn't for a party, though — Levi asked me if I wanted to go backpacking up on Mount Rainier on New Year's Eve. "It's Coach Hartwell's idea. We'll hike a few miles, spend the night up there, and then hike back the next day. It'll be great — just the mountain, the stars, the snow, and us."

Levi seemed to vibrate at the thought. For him, a hike like that would be a religious experience, but to me it just sounded cold. I'd never backpacked in the snow in my life, and my California coat was barely warm enough for Seattle's winter. I'd definitely need something warmer for Mount Rainier.

"What about storms?" I asked.

"The forecast is good, but if it changes we won't go. Mountains have no mercy."

"Let me think about it."

Levi looked disappointed, but then his face cheered up. "Is it equipment? Because I've got extra clothes and an extra winter sleeping bag. I'll be glad to lend them to you."

"No, it's not that, or not entirely that, though I would need to borrow stuff. I have to check with my dad first. He's been having me do some insulation work. He might want me to finish before school starts up again." That little lie gave me some breathing space — Levi would always finish work for his father before he did anything with me.

The more I thought about the camping trip, the less I liked it. Backpacking on a warm day in the summer had been fine, but trudging in the freezing cold through the snow sounded miserable. Besides, Levi and Hartwell were far more at home in the mountains than I was, so I'd slow them down. I hate being bad at anything athletic.

I called Levi at his home that night. "My dad wants me to finish in the basement," I said, which was partly true. "When you come back, you'll have to show me your drawings." Then an idea came to me. "Why don't you ask DeShawn or Brindle or one of the other guys?"

The weather was good on New Year's Eve — cold but crystal clear. Mount Rainier rose up out of the clouds in the southeast. I spent the evening alone watching NBA basketball in the den while my mother read in the living room. Every once in a while, I'd think about Levi and Hartwell looking at a sky filled with a million stars, and I'd half wish I was there with them.

11

ON TUESDAY SCHOOL STARTED UP again. Levi wasn't ready when I stopped by his house that morning, which wasn't like him. I waited, and as we hurried to Harding High, I asked him how the backpacking trip had gone.

"Okay."

"Anybody else from the team go along?" I asked.

"No."

"Did it snow?"

"Not much."

"Were there a lot of other backpackers?"

"No."

"Did you do some drawings?"

"No."

"Why not?"

"I just didn't."

After that, I didn't ask any more questions. What was the point? I was glad to get inside Harding High, so I could go my own way. As Levi walked off, his shoulders were slumped and his head was down.

Something was wrong.

We didn't hook up again until health class. I thought that by then he'd be back to his normal self, but he was still glum. When class ended, we shuffled out of the classroom and into the gym like death-row prisoners marching to the electric chair. That feeling wasn't new for me, but it was for him.

As usual, Knecht started practice with basic drills. Working on fundamentals is boring, but I had to admit that all the guys were dribbling better, passing better, playing better defense than they had been at the start of the year—and that included me. Knecht's stress on nuts and bolts had made us better players. If he'd just let us play fast, I'd have been okay with him as a coach.

After we finished the drills, we had a full-court scrimmage with Hartwell as the referee. Knecht sat along the sidelines at half-court, getting to his feet only if he saw something he didn't like.

We'd been going strong for ten minutes when it happened. Cash missed a shot, and my team rebounded. As I headed up-court, my feet got tangled up with Brindle's, and I ended up sprawled out on the ground. Then, as I was scrambling to my feet, somebody stepped on the back of my shoe and it came completely off.

I tried to pull the shoe back on, but I'd laced it tightly. The only thing to do was unlace it and start over. I knelt down, half looking at my shoe and half looking at the play unfolding at the other end of the court.

I was looking up, and then down, then up, so I didn't see everything. This I do know. Brandon Taylor, a second-string guy on my team, drove the lane and tossed up a wild, off-balance shot. Somebody got the rebound and cleared it to Brindle. "Go!" Hartwell shouted, and Brindle raced up-court toward me.

Panicked, I looked down at my shoe, trying to finish lacing it quickly so I could play defense. My head came up when I heard Knecht rasp out, "No, no!"

What followed played out like a slow-motion scene in a film. Hartwell had turned and was racing along the sideline to keep up with the fast break. Knecht, motioning to Brindle to slow down the play, came out of his chair along the sideline and stepped forward onto the court. Hartwell must not have seen Knecht, because he kept coming. I shouted: "Watch out!" but it was too late. Hartwell smacked into Knecht like an NFL safety smacks into a wide receiver. Knecht flew in the air before going down hard, his head making a sickening thud as it crashed against the hardwood court. His wire-rim glasses flew off and skittered across the gym floor, tumbling and turning until they came to a stop two feet from me.

Knecht lay twisted like a pretzel and perfectly still, so still I was afraid he was dead. Hartwell stared down at Knecht, and then Hartwell looked toward me. Our eyes locked for an instant, and we looked hard at one another, as if we were sharing a dark, unspoken secret. Then we both looked away. A second later the gym, which had fallen deathly silent, filled with noise. "Quick," Hartwell yelled, "somebody call 911."

Brindle raced to his gym bag and pulled out a cell phone. Hartwell leaned over Knecht and laid his head against the old man's chest. "He's breathing," Hartwell said to nobody and everybody. "Levi, help me get him onto his side. Cash, grab that sweatshirt and put it under his head. The rest of you, find stuff to lay on top of him to keep him warm."

Hartwell positioned Knecht so his hips and knees were at a sharp angle to one another. Next, he tilted Knecht's head back to make it easier for him to breathe. Hartwell checked his pulse, and then stared into his glazed eyes. "Hang in there, Coach," he whispered. "Hang in there."

In the far distance, a siren wailed.

We stayed huddled around Knecht as the siren grew louder. After what seemed like forever, the wailing stopped. A long minute later, the gym doors burst open and paramedics came rushing across the gym.

Hartwell stepped aside as they got to work. Two of them put Knecht on a stretcher while the third asked Hartwell what had happened, taking notes as he did.

Then they picked up the stretcher and carefully carried Knecht out. The gym doors swung shut behind them, and we turned back to Hartwell. For a moment he stared at us, confused. Then he pulled himself together.

"Practice is over. I'll follow the ambulance to the hospital. I've got your e-mail addresses on your health forms. I'll send a message out as soon as I learn anything. Right now, the only thing any of us can do is pray."

Back home I had trouble eating, trouble studying, trouble doing anything other than check my e-mail, which I did every five minutes. I kept seeing Knecht's crumpled body. He'd looked so old, so small.

Early in the evening, all I felt was worry and sorrow, but as the hours passed, other thoughts crept in, thoughts I couldn't push away no matter how hard I tried. I wanted Knecht to be all right, but it would be better for me if he couldn't come back. Hartwell would take over as head coach, and he'd make me the starting point guard. Half the season remained. If I got minutes, I could still put up decent numbers, numbers that would impress Coach Richter. Richter had told me that he wouldn't make a final decision until March or maybe even April. After my miserable start to the season, getting the scholarship was a long shot, but with Hartwell as head coach I'd have a chance, especially if I could turn the season around and lead Harding High into the playoffs.

Around ten the e-mail message from Hartwell finally came, addressed to everyone on the team: *"Coach Knecht has suffered a concussion, a broken hip, and a fractured collarbone. The injuries are serious, but his vital signs are stable. Keep praying. Coach Hartwell."*

What did it mean? My mom was home, so I printed Hartwell's e-mail, went downstairs, and showed it to her. "Oh my God," she said, putting her hand to her mouth. "The broken hip alone could kill him."

I was stunned. "You can die from a broken hip?"

She nodded. "He'll need surgery, which is dangerous for someone his age. And even if the surgery goes well, there's danger of an infection or pneumonia or a blood clot. A broken hip is very, very serious."

12

WHEN I STOPPED BY LEVI'S house before school the next morning, his sister Rachel told me he'd gone in early. He'd done that a few times before, but he'd always said something to me beforehand. I looked around for him in the halls before the first bell, but couldn't find him. I didn't see him until health class, but he came in late so there was no time to talk.

An intercom announcement at the end of the day directed varsity basketball players to meet in the library. "Coach Knecht is still in the hospital," Hartwell said, his voice somber, once we were all assembled. "I'm canceling today's practice. I don't have the heart for it, and I'm sure you don't, either." He motioned toward a table by the bank of computers. "You'll find a sheet of butcher paper over there. I thought that each of you could write something for Coach, and then I'll bring it to him. Hearing from you will mean a lot to him."

We shuffled over to the table and formed a haphazard line. Cash picked up the black marker first and wrote something. Brandon, who was like Levi in the respect he showed Knecht, went next. Levi printed: *I'm praying for you, —Levi.*

I took the pen from Levi and wrote: *"Get well soon."* My phrase seemed idiotic, but nobody else had done much better. Once every player had written something, Levi found a blank space and drew a perfect backboard with a perfect rim and a perfect net.

We played Saturday night against Inglemoor, our first game with Hartwell as head coach. The pregame locker room felt strange. When it was time to head onto the court, Hartwell had us stick our hands into a circle for a moment of silence. After that, no one knew what to do. Should we roar encouragement to one another, or would that be disrespectful to Coach Knecht? In the end we stayed silent, heading to the court as if we were headed to a math test.

Hartwell seemed unsure how to coach. He started Brindle at point guard and sat me on the bench, but in the huddle he told the guys to run. "Play the way we played against Garfield in the fourth quarter."

It made no sense. *I'd* been the point guard in the fourth quarter, not Brindle. If we were going to run, then Hartwell should have started me.

Brindle tried, but fast-break basketball isn't his style. When he did push the ball, which wasn't often, he produced more turnovers than buckets. Most of the time he ran Knecht's plays, even though Hartwell kept yelling at him to play fast.

With two minutes left in the first quarter, Hartwell subbed me into the game. For those two minutes, I tried to push the tempo, but I failed. For one thing, Levi had no energy, no fight. The guy he was guarding was out-hustling him for rebounds and loose balls, and I'd never seen anybody out-hustle Levi. But it wasn't just Levi; everybody was out of sync. It was as if we felt guilty to be playing, as if we were afraid to win.

Hartwell had Brindle play all but a couple of minutes in the second and third quarters — exactly duplicating Knecht's rotation. Brindle would make a few good plays, and we'd cut into Inglemoor's lead. A turnover would follow, or a couple of missed shots, and their lead would balloon back up to six or eight. On the sideline, Hartwell would holler directions, and then go quiet for long stretches. When the third quarter ended, we were down seven.

Hartwell put me in for Brindle to start the fourth quarter. The horn sounded, and we started toward the court. Then, behind me, I heard Hartwell yell: "Time-out, ref! Time-out." No coach ever calls time-out between quarters. Hartwell had had two full minutes to talk to us. What was he doing?

As we huddled around him, he dropped to a knee and looked up into our eyes. "Listen, guys," he said, his voice somber. "I know how you're feeling, because I'm feeling it too. But ask yourself this. Would Coach Knecht be happy with our effort? Our energy? The best gift you can give Coach Knecht is to play hard." He paused, and his eyes went from one player to the next. I was last, and his eyes were focused on me when he said: "Win it for Coach."

Inglemoor had possession to start the quarter. They came down, worked the ball inside, but their big guy was short on a turnaround jumper. Levi rebounded and hit me with an outlet. I raced into forecourt; it was a three-on-three situation, and my guy sagged off me, daring me to shoot.

I stepped back, went up for a fifteen-foot jumper, and the instant I released the ball, I knew it was a terrible shot. The ball caught the front of the rim, took a strange high bounce in the air, but somehow came down through the net. It was such a laughably lucky shot that that's what I did: I looked at my teammates and laughed. Cash, DeShawn, Nick — their eyes also gleamed with the absurdity of the shot. Even Levi smiled a little.

With that shot, the weight that had been holding us down was lifted. Inglemoor inbounded, and our defensive pressure was so intense that they struggled to get a play going. With the shot clock about to expire, their forward tossed up a hook that missed badly. DeShawn cleared the board and hit me in stride with a great outlet. I raced downcourt, pulled up at the free-throw line, and drained another jumper — this one a perfect swish. "That's it! That's it!" Hartwell shouted from the bench. "Push! Push! Push!"

On Inglemoor's next possession, DeShawn trapped his man in the corner. The guy panicked, twisting this way and that, and finally dragged his pivot foot, turning the ball over to us. While he whined to the ref, I broke up-court, drove the lane, and then kicked the ball out to Cash in the corner for the open three. His shot came from the exact spot where he'd missed earlier in the game, but this time the ball found nothing but net.

Once, when I was little, my mother was driving on Skyline Boulevard late at night. The road was so dark and empty that I was a little spooked. Then, from nowhere, a sports car — maybe a Ferrari or a Lamborghini, flew by us, passing us and then disappearing in a blur around the next bend. Against Inglemoor in the fourth quarter, we were the sports car flying by; all they saw were our taillights.

We won by nine.

I was so ecstatic when I reached the locker room that I wanted to let out a rock concert howl, but just in time I remembered Knecht lying in the hospital. Still, our locker room bubbled with excited talk. It was the Garfield win all over again, but this time everyone knew that Hartwell wouldn't hand the point guard job back to Brindle. I was Hartwell's guy.

Brindle knew it too. When we were both dressed, he came over to me and told me I'd played great. Then he stood tall and looked me in the eye. "I'm going to fight to get my starting spot back." We bumped knuckles, each of us respecting the other guy, and then he walked back to his locker.

The stat sheet came in as I finished lacing my shoes. I'd had eight points, six assists, and only one turnover. One negative thing jumped off the page at me. The basket Levi scored in the fourth quarter was his only hoop of the game. He had no blocked shots and his rebounds were also way down.

13

B ACK HOME, I E-MAILED COACH Richter, describing both the Inglemoor game and my promotion to first team. I didn't mention Coach Knecht's fall, I guess because I wanted Richter to think I'd earned the spot. It wasn't exactly a lie—I *had* earned it. I'd actually earned it twice—with my performance against Garfield and now with the game I'd had against Inglemoor.

I slept late on Sunday and in the afternoon I met with Celia to study for the chemistry final. I knew exactly what would be on the test, but I let Celia lead the study session so she wouldn't become suspicious, which meant the time dragged. When we finally finished, we talked for a few minutes and then she stood up to go. "This really helped," she said as she gathered together her stuff. "You're a good study partner, Jonas."

I mumbled some sort of answer all the while feeling like one of those insects that hide under rocks. When she was gone, I vowed never to cheat again on anything.

Hartwell started Monday's practice with an update on Coach Knecht's condition. The old guy was improving, but he was still in the hospital. The room fell quiet for a long moment, but then we got to work.

Hartwell had written our remaining games on the white board in the locker room. "Garfield is the top team in this state, and we beat them. That's the good news. The bad news is that we've lost a bunch of games we should have won. Remember, though, it's only January. We can still win enough games to make the KingCo District tournament. Once we make the playoffs, the regular season goes out the window." He held up his hand. "If we play separately, then we're weak like these five fingers. But if we play together" — he clenched his fingers into a fist — "we're strong."

With that, Hartwell sent us onto the court for practice. While we warmed up, he plugged his iPod into the gym's sound system. A second later the gym filled with loud rap music. Cash looked at me, grinned, and fired off a shot; Nick did the same.

The Knecht era was over.

Once we were loose, we went straight to scrimmaging — no drills, no practicing set plays, none of that Knecht stuff. A fast up-and-down game was what Hartwell wanted, and that meant running, running, and more running.

I had gotten Levi to talk to me some before and after health class and during warm-ups, though his voice had been cheerless. And on the basketball court, he was still out of sync. Toward the end of practice, Cash threw him a great pass that should have resulted in any easy bucket. Instead, Levi fumbled it out-of-bounds. "Come on, Double D," Cash said, getting up into his face, "you've got to make that play." It was the first time in weeks anybody had called him "Double D."

I expected Levi to drop his head and mutter that he was

sorry — that's what he always did when he screwed up a play and somebody got on him. This time he reached out, grabbed Cash by the jersey, and yanked him forward. "Don't call me 'Double D,'" he hissed, his eyes malicious.

DeShawn jumped in then and so did Nick, pulling them apart. As DeShawn pulled Cash away, Cash put on a show, screaming that he was ready to fight any time, any place. Levi stared him down, fists clenched. Hartwell, who'd been watching from ten rows up in the bleachers, came bounding down. "That's enough," he said as he reached the court. "Save it for Woodinville."

For the last twenty minutes of practice, I could feel how close Levi was to exploding. For months I'd be waiting for him to stand up against the "Double D" stuff. Now that he done it, I wasn't sure how I felt. The guy with the clenched fists and the eyes filled with hatred wasn't the Levi I'd known.

14

E BLEW OPEN THE WOODINVILLE game in the second quarter when our defense forced four straight turnovers leading to four straight buckets. We were up six when the run started, and two minutes later we were up fourteen.

If you keep pushing the ball at a team that just wants the game to be over, your lead grows and grows. When the margin reached twenty-five early in the third quarter, I figured Hartwell would either put in the second string or tell us to back off. He did neither. "Keep running!" he said during a time-out, his voice urgent as if the game were close. "Bury these guys." When the horn sounded ending the game, the score was 83–46.

Our Friday game against the Hale Raiders figured to be tougher. Their best player, a shooting guard named Lucius Jackson, had gotten a scholarship to USC and was a cinch for all-league selection. Cash couldn't handle him alone, so we practiced a bunch of double-team rotations. Still, I could see Hartwell was worried.

At game time, though, we caught a break. Jackson had broken a team rule, and as punishment his coach benched him for the first half. When Jackson entered the game at the start of the second half, we were up ten points. The guy obviously had the tools, but sitting the first half had kept him out of the flow, or maybe he was mad at his coach over the benching. Twice he didn't hustle after loose balls, and when he loafed a third time, Hale's coach sent him to the end of the bench. Jackson never returned, and Hale never made a run at us. We won by sixteen.

In the locker room after both games, guys devoured the stat sheet, smiling as they saw their soaring numbers. When you play fast-break basketball, points come in bundles. The only player who had struggled was Levi.

I had my mom's car that night, and after the Hale game, Levi and I drove back to Tangletown. He didn't talk; instead, he stared out the window into the blackness. From the way he looked — mouth tight, brow furrowed — anyone would have thought we'd lost by fifty. A couple of times I'd say something, and he'd sit up. "What?" he'd ask, his mind somewhere else. I'd repeat whatever I'd said only to get a one-word reply. Finally I gave up and just drove.

As we neared his house, I tried one last time. "Everything okay? At home, I mean. Your parents? Your sisters? Anything going on you want to talk about?"

He wheeled on me. "Why would you ask something like that?"

"I don't know. You're getting passing grades; we're winning, but you don't seem to be enjoying anything. I know Coach Knecht is on your mind, but if something else is wrong somewhere, and you ever feel like talking about it . . ." I stopped, not sure how to say what I wanted to say. "I guess I'm just saying I'm your friend."

"Nothing's wrong, Jonas," he replied, the edge gone from his voice, but then he turned away from me to stare out the window again.

I was worried about Levi for Levi's sake, but I was worried about him for me, too. In his e-mails, Coach Richter stressed that team results were more important to him than individual statistics. Making the playoffs would extend our season and give me more chances to impress Richter. But the team couldn't keep winning without Levi playing like Levi — not against the tough teams that were coming up. Something besides Knecht was holding him back. If I couldn't get him turned around, that *something* — whatever it was — would hold me back, too.

15

OUR SUCCESS GOT NOTICED. WHEN I came downstairs the morning after the Hale game, my dad handed me the *Seattle Times*. "You'll want to read that article," he said, pointing to the headline:

HARDING HAWKS RALLY FOR INJURED COACH

The story started with a description of Mr. Knecht's injury, before recapping his career. Most of the information was new to me. Knecht had been Seattle Coach of the Year three times. Twice in the 1980s Harding had played for the state title, losing both games. At the end of the article, the writer quoted Hartwell: "The team has dedicated the season to Coach Knecht. We're playing for him, one game at a time, the way he'd have us play."

I read those last sentences twice. Nobody — not Hartwell, not Levi, not Cash — had said anything about dedicating the season to Knecht, and we definitely weren't playing Knecht's style. I didn't exactly blame Hartwell for saying what he'd said — it was what was expected. Still, it didn't sit quite right.

After beating Inglemoor and then stomping on Woodinville

and Hale, I wasn't worried about Monday's game with Eastlake. They had a decent record but nothing sensational and, as the *Times* had said, we were a team on the rise.

As my mom gave me the keys to her car that morning, she wished me luck.

"We're not going to need luck this time. We can handle these guys."

"Don't be too sure of yourself."

"You sound like Dad," I said, and then I was out the door.

The Eastlake game was part of the Martin Luther King Jr. Holiday Hoops celebration at KeyArena, which had been home to the Sonics when they played in Seattle. I thought I'd feel an extra burst of adrenaline when I stepped onto the same court where Michael Jordan and other great NBA stars had played, but it didn't happen. Our game was the first of the day, with a tip-off time of ten in the morning. When the horn sounded and we took the court, over fifteen thousand seats were empty. I felt like we were playing in a warehouse. The hour didn't feel right, either; ten was way too early to do anything other than shoot around.

We jumped out to an early lead. A couple of times I thought we'd get our fast break going and deliver a knockout blow, but Eastlake hung tough, mainly because of their depth. The Eastlake coach also had his team play fast, but he ran ten players out against us, and those ten split the minutes evenly. Hartwell used seven, and our subs only spotted us a minute or two. The Eastlake players' legs stayed fresh while ours grew heavy.

Coach Knecht would have had us walk the ball down, milk the clock, and rest a little on offense so we'd be strong on defense — but Hartwell told us to keep running. We did, but our increasing fatigue made our execution sloppy. Eastlake took advantage, chipping away at our lead. At halftime the game was tied.

During the break, we caught our breath and came out strong in the third quarter, jumping out to a decent lead. Again the Eastlake coach substituted freely, always shuffling rested players onto the court. Hartwell, who had no faith in our bench guys, made even fewer substitutions, but he kept telling us to run every chance we had.

By the end of the third quarter, I was so winded I was leaning over and sucking in air, my hands on my knees, as Hartwell barked instructions. I looked around the huddle and saw Levi, Cash, and DeShawn bent over too. Nick had dropped to a knee. It would have been good coaching to give us a couple of minutes of rest, but Hartwell sent the entire first team onto the court to start the final quarter. "Gut it out," he screamed. "You can't let yourself be tired, not now."

That mind-over-matter talk sounds good, but midway through the fourth quarter, we hit the wall — all of us. Once your legs go rubbery, your shots come up short, and you stop blocking out on rebounds. You don't move your feet, which makes you foul-prone. Eastlake gnawed into our lead like a dog working on a bone.

When we most needed some breaks, calls started going against us. If one of us plowed into an Eastlake player, it was a charge, and they got the ball. But if their guy smacked into us, the ref called a blocking foul and they shot free throws.

The worst call came at the worst time. We were up by a single point with thirty seconds to play when Eastlake's forward missed a jumper. In the fight for the rebound, an Eastlake guy tipped the ball out-of-bounds, but the ref saw it the other way, giving the ball back to Eastlake. On the inbound play, their center flashed into the key, took the pass, and banked in an eight-footer over Levi that gave Eastlake the lead.

We had twenty seconds left, and we were down one. Score a hoop and we'd pull out a victory. Hartwell called time and drew up a play straight out of Knecht's playbook. We were to go into a weave, have Nick set a screen, and then have Cash come off the screen for a jump shot.

It worked: Cash flashed open; I hit him in rhythm. He got a good look at the hoop, released, and missed short — those tired legs again. Then we finally caught a break — the rebound came straight to Levi. He dribbled once, gathered himself, gave a shoulder fake, and rose for what should have been the winning basket. But as he left his feet, an Eastlake guard slapped at the ball. He was a little guy, and he shouldn't have been able to knock the ball out of Levi's strong hands, but the ball came loose and rolled toward the sideline. I dived for it, and so did everybody else. While we fumbled it around, the horn sounded, ending the game.

In the locker room afterward, I knew why we lost, knew it in the weariness I felt. They'd come at us in droves, and they'd worn us down. But the stat sheet revealed a second reason: Levi. He'd managed only three points and three rebounds. Had we gotten anything close to a normal game from him, we would have won easily.

16

AT THE START OF ENGLISH class on Tuesday, the phone rang in Mrs. Miller's classroom. The interruption came just as we'd begun discussing a poem by Robert Frost, her favorite writer. When she hung up the telephone, she scowled and told me to report to Coach Hartwell's office. "If this is about basketball, then I don't like it one bit. You get yourself back here as soon as you can."

My new basketball shoes squeaked loudly as I walked alone down the empty hallways. When I reached Hartwell's office, I tapped lightly. "Come in, Jonas," he said as he opened the door. "This will just take a couple of minutes."

He returned to the seat behind his desk while I settled into a chair across from him. He had a frown on his face; the Eastlake loss was eating at him too. "I brought you in here because I just got off the phone with your New Hampshire coach."

I sat up, my heart suddenly thumping.

Hartwell put his hands up to let me know there was no real news. "I called to tell him what a fine player you are, what a fine person you are, and how you'd be great for his team. I also explained why you were on the bench for the first half of the season. I wanted him to hear it directly from me."

"Thanks, Coach. I appreciate it." I paused. "Did he say anything about my chances?"

Hartwell looked directly at me, his eyes searching out mine. "He told me that he's leaning toward the other boy. You'll need a strong finish to your season, but you're still in the running. I want him to see how well you're playing, so I've arranged with Mr. Clark to have one of his students film our next few games. He'll make a DVD of your highlights that you can send off to New Hampshire. Mr. Knecht should have done this for you, but better late than never. Is that okay with you?"

"Yeah, sure. My coach last year did that."

The room went silent. Was that it? I almost stood to leave, but somehow I sensed Hartwell had more to say, so I waited. He moved some papers around on his desk and then looked back to me. "I wouldn't normally speak to one player about another player, but I'd like to believe that we're friends, that I can speak with you in confidence."

I swallowed. "The other player is Levi, right?"

He nodded. "Yes, Levi. He's been skipping our tutoring sessions, and his play on the court has been way off. I'm worried about him."

My chest tightened. I dropped my eyes. "Something's eating at him, Coach. I've tried to get him to tell me what it is, but whenever I ask, he shuts down."

Hartwell folded his hands. "Do you have any idea what it might be?"

"I think it might have to do with his sister Rachel. I know she fights with his father, but that's just a guess."

"So he hasn't told you anything?"

"No. Nothing."

Hartwell unfolded his hands and the tension left his face. "Well, whatever the reason, if Levi does poorly in class, he'll lose his eligibility. That's what happened to him last year. And even if he does manage to stay eligible, we have no chance against a team like Garfield unless he gets some passion back in his game."

I squirmed. Was Hartwell blaming me? "I've asked what's bothering him," I said. "He won't tell me. I don't know what else I can do."

Hartwell waved his hands in front of his face. "Jonas, I don't expect you to do anything. But with your permission, I'd like to explain to Levi just how important it is for us to make the playoffs. If Levi understands that you need to play more games and put up some numbers to win that scholarship, he just might shake off whatever is bothering him and bring some fire back. It's a win-win-win situation: good for you, good for him, and good for the team." Hartwell paused. "So what do you say? Can I explain to him how much these games mean to you?"

I didn't answer at first. Something about Hartwell's proposal didn't sound right, but how can it be wrong to ask a guy to play hard? "Okay," I said at last. "Just make sure to let him know it won't be his fault if Monitor College picks the other guy."

"I won't make him feel guilty," Hartwell said. "That wouldn't help his play at all. And Jonas, don't feel like you have to be the one to solve Levi's problems. He's got his parents, he's got his church, and he's on my radar screen. You take care of yourself and let the adults unravel whatever is bothering Levi."

I nodded, relieved. I stood and started for the door.

"One more thing," Hartwell said.

I turned back.

He smiled. "At practice today I'm going to tell the guys that you're co-captain of the team. Don't worry. I checked with Cash, and he's all for it."

17

HARTWELL MUST HAVE TALKED TO Levi about my scholarship sometime during that school day, because Levi worked hard at practice that afternoon. He wasn't the old Levi — there was no smile on his face or joy in his game — but the focus was back, and he played angry, which is a good way for a power forward to play.

Semester finals were the first week of February, so there were no games during that week. Our last game before the break was on Friday night against Skyline in their gym. We needed to get back on track after the Eastlake loss, but Skyline was a perennial playoff team. Winning wouldn't be easy. My dad left me a note on the kitchen table. *"Get these guys!"* it read.

Before the game, the Skyline players were cocky, shooting long three-pointers, joking with one another, acting as if we weren't worthy to be on the court with them. They were taking us lightly, probably because they knew we'd lost to Eastlake, a team they'd routed twice. But after we got off to a blistering start — scoring the first eight points of the game — their cockiness disappeared.

Their coach called time-out. As we huddled around Hartwell, we could hear the other coach chewing out his players. When they came back on the court, their approach changed entirely. Instead of firing up long jumpers, they pounded the ball inside.

To hold them off, we needed Levi, and for the first time in a long time, he was there. On defense he clogged the middle, blocked shots, and rebounded. When we were on offense, I didn't involve him too much. A player has only so much energy; Levi was expending his on the other end of the court. Time and again, Skyline would make mini-runs at us, but Levi would have a great block, Cash would hit a three, or I'd sneak in for a lay-up, and we'd maintain our lead.

Midway through the fourth quarter, we were up by six points. Hartwell had subbed more, learning from his mistake against Eastlake, so we weren't exhausted. As long as we kept our composure, we'd win — or at least that's what I thought.

Then, in a matter of seconds, everything changed. DeShawn missed a jumper; Skyline rebounded and came downcourt. Instead of setting up a play, Skyline's point guard — a guy I'd had under control all game long — let fly a twenty-five-footer. He was way out of his range; it would have been an NBA three-pointer. I turned, ready to rebound, but to the astonishment of everybody in the gym, the ball whistled through. The Skyline crowd, electrified, rose to their feet and roared. In the blink of an eye, our lead had been cut in half.

You can taste fear when you're playing, and that's the taste that came to my mouth. I brought the ball into forecourt, the roar from the fans growing louder and louder: "DE-FENSE! DE-FENSE! DE-FENSE!" We worked the ball around, with nobody panicking. With ten seconds left on the shot clock, Nick flashed open. I hit him with a solid chest pass. He went up in rhythm, but the crowd noise had gotten into his head. Instead of releasing the ball, he guided it. His shot was flat and short; Skyline's center pounced on the rebound, made a quick outlet, and they were racing downcourt again.

This time my guy pulled up and let his shot fly from about thirty feet. The second he let it go, I knew — everyone knew. The crowd, which had been holding its breath while that rainbow came down from the sky, erupted.

Swish!

The score was tied with three minutes to play.

Hartwell jumped up, signaling for a time-out. "Use the weave," he said as we huddled around him. "Just like Coach Knecht taught you. Milk the clock and get a good shot."

Our time-out quieted Skyline's crowd a little, and so did our set play. Skyline's fans still chanted, "DE-FENSE," but not with the same crazy intensity. As the shot clock wound down, we moved the ball around the perimeter. Then Levi's eyes caught mine. He hadn't shown any offense all game, so Skyline wasn't expecting anything from him. A second after our eyes met, he went backdoor, and I put up a lob near the rim. It wasn't a great pass, but he snatched the ball and kissed it off the glass and through. A whistle sounded — foul on Skyline. Levi calmly sank the free throw, and we were back up by three.

After the inbound pass, I got up into the face of the Skyline guard — I was not going to let him sink another three-pointer. I rode him downcourt, giving him no look at the hoop at all. Still, he rose and heaved up another long bomb. He must have figured he was so hot that nothing could stop him, but this time his shot fell five feet short and right into Cash's waiting hands. I had released downcourt, and Cash heaved the ball to me. I took it on a bounce, made the lay-up, and the game was ours.

Afterward, I studied the stat sheet. My line was a thing of beauty: ten points and ten assists. A double-double — something that doesn't happen much in high school basketball, and something that would definitely catch Richter's attention. So would the 5–1 record the team had with me as a starter. Most importantly, we'd moved one step closer to earning a spot in the KingCo playoffs.

My eyes drifted down the page to Levi's name. He had seven points, four blocks, and twelve rebounds — by far his best game in weeks. He was lacing up his shoes on the other side of the locker room. I thought about shouting, *Great game, Levi,* and waving the stat page around, but that wasn't Levi's way, and it wasn't exactly mine, either.

18

MY SCHEDULE DURING FINALS WEEK was confusing. There were "A" days and "B" days, lunches as early as ten in the morning or as late as one in the afternoon.

Levi's schedule was equally muddled. I wanted to review the health notes with him early in the week to make sure I got it done before I studied for my harder classes. In the hall before school on Monday, I asked him what time would be good. "How about after practice today?" he said.

Even though we wouldn't play our next game until Saturday night, Hartwell didn't go easy on us at practice. "This is going to feel more like a track meet than a basketball practice," he said that afternoon. "When we start tournament play, we'll be facing tough games one night after the next. KingCo runs Thursday, Friday, with the championship on Sunday. Once we win that and go to the state finals, we'll be looking at three more games, but this time it will be three games in only three nights. I'm going to wear you out now so you're not tired then, and I don't want to hear any whining."

I liked that Hartwell had acted as if he was certain we'd win KingCo one week and then progress to the state finals the next.

He was playing a mind game with us, but it always feels good to have a coach give you a vote of confidence.

That was by far the toughest practice of my life. We ran and ran and then ran more. After fifty minutes I was dripping sweat, and the second half of practice was harder than the first.

Afterward, Levi and I went straight to the library, pulled out our health notes, and got to it. Predictably, Levi thought he needed to learn absolutely everything, but he trusted me when I told him he could let some things go. After forty-five minutes, he'd mastered more than he needed to pass.

"How are you doing in your other classes?" I asked.

He roughly shoved his books into his backpack. "Don't worry, Jonas. I'll work with Hartwell enough to keep myself eligible. I won't let you down."

There was a buried anger to his tone that made no sense. I thought about calling him on it, but then remembered what Hartwell had said about not trying to do too much. Instead, I punched him on the shoulder. "When this is all over, how about if we go backpacking again?" I said, laughing.

It took a while, but finally he managed to smile back. "Sounds good, Jonas. Sounds really good."

19

TUESDAY MORNING I HAD STUDY period first thing, and I used it to check with Sam Fisher, the guy making the DVD of my highlights to send to Monitor College. Fisher, who was in my English class, was always talking about why one short story would make a good film while another one wouldn't. Film was for him what basketball was for me.

He showed me what he had done, which was to splice together segments showing me making great passes and sinking baskets. About five minutes into the DVD, he hit the Stop button. "The rest is pretty much the same. That's what you wanted, right?"

I shrugged. "I guess."

He woke up a little. "Don't you like it?"

"Do you?" I asked, not wanting to step on his toes.

"I think it's phony, but it's what Mr. Hartwell told me to do."

"What would make it better?"

"Including some plays you screw up. Show all your reactions, all your emotions. It'd be way more interesting, way more like a real film."

"Go for it," I said, recalling what Coach Russell at Redwood High had said about honesty.

Fisher's face broke into a big smile. "All right. I will."

Celia had asked to meet me at Zoka for a general study session. When practice ended that day — it was another long, hard workout — on an impulse I asked Levi if he wanted to come along.

"Other than health, I'm not in any of your classes," he said.

"That doesn't matter. You can go over your stuff while we're studying ours. It's easier to work when other people are around, and it's more fun."

"I'll think about it."

I ate a quick dinner and then went to Zoka. Celia and I spent an hour sipping hot chocolate, nibbling on pastries, and reviewing chemistry. I fought the impulse to nudge her toward the topics that were on the test and away from those that weren't. I was glad to finish with chemistry and turn to English and American government.

We didn't have the same teachers for those classes, but I asked Celia for advice anyway. "Keep your essays short," she said, "and make sure your paragraphs all have a topic sentence followed by supporting details. The surest way to get a lousy grade is to ramble on and on."

She studied her notes as I read through mine. Every once in a while the main door to Zoka would open. I'd look up, hoping to see Levi, but he never showed. At ten, Celia and I called it a night.

The chemistry test was first thing Wednesday morning. Butler passed out a packet of papers, and immediately the kids around me flipped ahead to see what was coming, fearing the worst. I did the same, even though there were no surprises for me. When I turned in the test, I knew I'd done well enough to get a B.

My last exam was Friday afternoon — American government. The essay question was about a man who'd stolen from an old woman's bank account, used the cash to win money at the racetrack, and then had returned every penny he'd stolen. The thief was caught, but his lawyer said he should be able to keep the racetrack winnings. I wrote that he should have to give up the money because he hadn't risked anything. The old woman was the person who stood to lose, I argued, so she should gain. I finished before anyone else, but every sentence was crystal clear, which is what Celia had insisted mattered most. I turned in my paper and then sat back down. Finals week was over.

20

WE PLAYED LAKESIDE ON SATURDAY night at home. It felt great to be able to concentrate on basketball again. Lakeside was no soft touch, but they weren't Garfield. Beat them, and we'd qualify for the KingCo tournament. We'd be a low seed, a seven or an eight, but we'd be in. Lose and our season was over.

Lakeside had one really good player — J. D. Lester — and the other guys were just out there. Lester was a slasher, six four with great ball-handling skills. His teammates set screens all over the court for him, trying to create mismatches. It was a good game plan — at the end of the first quarter we were tied, 11–11, and Lester had been sizzling hot, scoring nine of Lakeside's points.

He'd also played the entire quarter.

I felt good about our chances. He couldn't stay on fire for a full game, and there was nobody on his team to pick up the slack when he cooled.

"Make Lester work hard on defense too," Hartwell instructed. "Nick, he's guarding you most of the time. Be active. Keep moving, and take the shots that come your way. Make him run his butt off."

I kept waiting for Lester to cool off, but all through the second quarter, he stayed red-hot. He hit two three-pointers over Nick, and when Nick got up in his face, Lester drove by him for two lay-ups. What really had me worried was his breathing: the guy wasn't sucking air at all. At halftime we were down six.

And we were still down six at the end of the third quarter. Lester had cooled some, but Levi had been our only consistent threat, so they'd started to throw double-teams at him, forcing him to pass. We had good looks at the hoop, but all through the game Cash had been cold, and I wasn't exactly lighting it up, so Lakeside kept double-teaming Levi.

Eight minutes to save our season.

During the break between the third and fourth quarter, Hartwell kept running his hands through his hair. "Let your shots go," he pleaded. "You're short-arming them. Free and easy. Just relax."

When you're told to relax, it makes you more tense — or at least that's how it works for me. Just as we were about to head back onto the court, Levi spoke. "I can shut Lester down."

I was stunned; we all were. He'd never spoken up before in a huddle, but what he said made perfect sense. I remembered those summertime one-on-one games at the Good Shepherd Center. I'd had no chance against him. Lester was taller than I was, but he still wouldn't be able to shoot over Levi or drive past him.

Hartwell looked doubtful. "Lester's a guard; you're a forward. He's too quick for you."

"No, he isn't," Levi said, calm certainty in his voice.

The horn sounded; the ref stuck his head in. "Your players need to be on the court, Coach."

"It'll work," I said to Hartwell.

Hartwell chewed on his lip for a moment and then decided. "All right, we'll try it. Nick, you take Levi's spot underneath. Box out and you'll be okay. Levi, don't foul Lester on his jump shots. If he blows by you and is going to get an easy lay-up, a foul is okay, but not on the jump shot." The ref leaned in again. "Go!" Hartwell shouted before the ref spoke, and we hurried back onto the court.

Lakeside inbounded, and their point guard brought the ball up-court. Levi, almost casually, sidled over to Lester, but there was nothing casual about his defense once the ball was in the forecourt. Levi hounded him, doing everything to deny him the ball. When Lester finally got the ball, he was nearly at half-court. Levi backed off a little, but once Lester put the ball on the floor, Levi was back on him. After a few dribbles, Lester picked up his dribble and quickly passed the ball back to the point guard. Instantly Levi was up in his face, denying a return pass.

Lakeside didn't get off a shot on that possession, and Levi shut down Lester the rest of the way. Lester couldn't drive by him, couldn't shoot over him, couldn't do anything. As Lakeside's offense ground to a halt, we gained confidence. Cash missed his first shot of the fourth quarter, but nailed his next two. I made my first, and when I missed my second, DeShawn was there for the offensive rebound and the put-back.

We didn't race past Lakeside; we scratched and clawed our way past them, tying the game on a reverse lay-up by Cash with two minutes left — and taking the lead on our next possession when Levi hit a short jump hook. By then Lester had stopped trying to get the ball — Levi had thoroughly demoralized him.

Lakeside scored a grand total of four points in the fourth quarter, the final two coming with five seconds left.

We won, 60–54, clinching a spot in the playoffs.

We had a small celebration after the game, letting out a few shouts and pounding on a few lockers. Levi joined in — sort of. He smiled and high-fived guys, but he didn't look as if his heart was in it. I had my mom's car again, so I gave him a ride home. He was quiet in the car, which seemed normal now, staring out the window into the darkness.

He didn't speak until I pulled up in front of his house. "This will help, right?" he said before he got out of the car. "With your chance for the scholarship?"

"It sure will. I can tell the coach in New Hampshire we made the playoffs, and I'll have at least a few more games to score some points and make some assists. It wouldn't have happened without you, Levi."

We bumped knuckles then. "I'm glad for you, Jonas." Then he got out of the car and went into his house.

As soon as I was in my own room, I flipped open my laptop, e-mailed my stats to Coach Richter, and told him we'd made the playoffs. The next morning I had a return e-mail. "Congratulations. I'll be following the tournament online. When you go up against the best, you find out who you really are."

He didn't come right out and say that my scholarship depended on my performance in the playoffs.

He didn't have to.

21

LEARNED FROM THE MORNING *Seattle Times* that we wouldn't have to win the district tournament to make it into the state playoffs. Because of its large population, King County was awarded two teams in the final eight. If we could win our way into the final against Garfield — and they were sure to make it — we wouldn't have to beat them. Second place would be good enough.

On Tuesday Sam Fisher, the video guy, intercepted me on my way to the lunchroom. "Bring your food to the lab, and I'll show you the new version," he said.

I grabbed a burrito and hustled to the video room. Fisher hooked up his computer to a seventy-inch television, and we watched twenty minutes of a DVD starring me.

It was a strange experience. When I was actually on the court playing in games, I felt as if I were doing the same things that college players, even NBA players, do. But watching Fisher's film, my "laser" passes were just passes. On the big screen, I looked more like a scrawny eighth-grader than a muscular college player. I didn't complain, though. Fisher had done exactly what I'd wanted; Richter would get an accurate picture of me, good and bad.

After fifteen minutes, lunch period ended. "I used two games to put the film together," Fisher said, ejecting the DVD. "Thirty minutes total. Is that enough?"

"That's enough."

"Who's this for, anyway?" Fisher asked, as he handed me the DVD.

I explained about the scholarship.

"That's cool, Jonas. If you get it, tell me. I can brag to people that it was all because of my cinéma vérité style."

The first two games of the KingCo tournament went by in a blur. We beat Newcastle by eight and then were back on the court less than twenty-four hours later to take on Kentwood. In both games, everything clicked. Levi was controlling the boards; Cash was hitting his jump shot; I was distributing the ball. We jumped out to early leads and then Hartwell put Brindle in to milk the clock in the fourth quarter and to keep me fresh for the next game.

For the previous few weeks, my father had occasionally been leaving work before closing. That night he was reading the newspaper in the front room when I opened the door. "How did you do?" he said, nervousness in his voice. He hadn't been to my games, but he was following the results.

I gave him the details of our victory. "Even if we lose to Garfield Sunday night, we're still in the state tournament."

He wagged a finger at me. "You beat Garfield before. You shouldn't talk about losing."

I shrugged. "I know, but —"

"But even if you lose, you're still in the state tournament." He paused. "Congratulations. I can't tell you how proud I am."

There was a moment of silence. "How are things at the Blue Jay?" I asked.

"Going great. I'm feeling good about my new cleanup supervisor. I've finally got a guy who understands how important cleanliness is. I may end up having both a job and a life."

"Can you make the Garfield game?"

"Your mom and I will both be there, and we'll be at your state championship game too. And for sure we'll make your first game in New Hampshire."

"Don't jinx me," I said. "I don't have the scholarship yet."

"You'll get it, Jonas. Just keep playing hard."

A couple of hours later, as I was lying in bed, I thought of Levi's father. Would he miss the championship game? But even as I asked myself the question, I knew the answer.

22

THE DISTRICT FINAL WAS HELD at Hec Edmundson Pavilion on the University of Washington campus. Garfield had a regional reputation, so their fans outnumbered ours. After going through our normal warm-up routine, we returned to the locker room. Hartwell had us line up in the runway, and then the gym went dark. The PA announcer called our names one by one. I ran out of the darkness into a bright spotlight, rock music blaring from the sound system. Cheers rolled down from our side of the stands. The hair on my arms stood up, and I thought my heart would come out of my chest.

I'd been playing well, but I knew I could play better. In Fisher's video, I'd seen times when I'd missed open teammates. Not once in Seattle had I gone into the zone like I had in Redwood City. I'd never had the feeling that the game was in slow motion — but sometimes it seemed as if that magical feeling was close.

After our team was introduced, the Garfield guys entered the arena the same way, except the cheering for them was louder. When the lights went fully on, I spotted the KingCo District trophy, three feet high and glittering, sitting on the scorer's table. Behind the scorer's table sat a line of reporters. Photographers ringed the court. I looked for my mom and dad in the packed stands, but there was no way I'd find them. If the KingCo championship game was this exciting, what would the state title game at the Tacoma Dome be like?

Garfield had three top-notch AAU players, guys who traveled the country in the summer playing against the best. The spotlight, the trophy, and the cameras — none of it seemed to faze them, but the pregame razzle-dazzle amped me up. I started the game playing too fast, trying to make miracle passes by threading the needle when my guy wasn't open. And when I wasn't making bad passes, I was taking bad shots. Twice I drove into the lane and threw up dipsy-doodle shots that caromed wildly off.

Garfield had a solid game plan. From the opening tip, they pounded the ball at Levi underneath. On every play at both ends of the court, somebody pushed him or gave him a forearm as they ran by. The refs let the first few bumps go, and once that happens, they have to let them all go.

Garfield took an early lead, but that didn't stop them from smacking Levi around. I could see anger rising in his eyes, a dangerous fury that would have surprised me a month ago but didn't surprise me now. I looked over at Hartwell. Did he see it?

In the second quarter, Garfield guys kept elbowing and shoving Levi, trying to get under his skin. He'd shoved back a couple of times and, as usually happens, the refs called fouls on him. That just increased his rage.

Garfield's lead was eight near the end of the quarter when Cash missed a jumper from the free-throw line. Levi was in position for the rebound, but a Garfield guy hit him from behind with a forearm that sent Levi into the first row of seats. It was an obvious foul, but the underneath ref must have been blocked from seeing it because he didn't blow his whistle. Levi righted himself, his face red with fury, and raced downcourt to play defense.

Garfield's guard, running the fast break, had held up briefly at the free-throw line before turning on the jets to drive to the hoop. Levi, coming full speed the length of the court, caught up with him just as the guy skied for the lay-up. While he was in the air, Levi smacked him — bringing his arm down hard on the guy's head.

The Garfield guard crashed to the ground, taking out a cameraman. Immediately a couple of the Garfield big guys went after Levi, and Levi stepped right up into their faces. Before he could throw a punch, I grabbed him and pulled him back. He tried to shrug me off like I was one of his sisters, but I hung on. The refs, blowing their whistles like madmen, jumped in front of the Garfield guys. Hartwell raced onto the court and helped me drag Levi to the bench. The biggest of the Garfield guys pointed his finger at Levi. "This isn't over!" he shouted. "This isn't over!"

The refs gave Levi both a personal foul and a technical foul. Garfield's point guard made three free throws to stretch their lead to eleven. The halftime horn sounded a few seconds later. As we traipsed, heads down, to the locker room, it was hard to believe that an hour before we'd been high on an adrenaline rush.

In the second half, Garfield ran the clock down on most possessions, but took the fast break if it was there. Hartwell kept Levi on the bench all through the third quarter but put him back in the game to begin the fourth quarter. There was some pushing and shoving on both sides, but Garfield was up by twenty and closing in on a trophy—they didn't need to fight.

When the game ended, our side of the gym was half empty. I spotted my dad, and he shook his head. Garfield had beaten us by nineteen, letting every team in Washington know that their earlier loss to us—their only loss all season—had been a fluke. They were going to take the state finals; the rest of us were playing for second.

In the locker room, Hartwell tried to keep up our spirits. "Think where we were a month ago compared to where we are now. We've fought our way into the state tournament. We've still got a shot at a bigger trophy than the one that got away today. Remember that."

When I reached home, my dad was back at the Blue Jay, but my mom was waiting for me, her eyes cheerful. "I know you're disappointed, Jonas, but you tried your best. That's all you can do."

I nodded, and she kissed me on the forehead. I moved past her toward the stairs.

"Jonas?"

I turned back.

"What happened with Levi tonight? I didn't know he had such a temper."

"Things like that happen. It's part of the game."

"It's never been part of Levi's game. Is something wrong?"

"Nothing's wrong."

"Well, he'd better get his temper under control. He could have seriously hurt that boy. Your father says he should have been ejected from the game."

23

ICHTER HAD E-MAILED ME AFTER each of our tournament victories — the *Seattle Times* was printing recaps and stats so he could follow everything online. He'd see that Garfield had wiped us out, and that I'd done nothing. Would he know that Garfield guys were headed to major colleges? I was almost positive he would.

Almost.

Monday morning I stopped by Levi's house on the way to Harding. "He left twenty minutes ago," his father said. I turned to leave when his father reached out and grabbed my shoulder, which I didn't like. "My daughter Rachel," he said, motioning toward her as she stood behind him getting ready to head out the door. "Does she wear immodest clothes at school?"

Rachel looked over his shoulder at me, panic in her eyes. She was wearing a baggy sweatshirt and sweatpants. I'd never once seen her at school in anything but low-cut tops and skintight jeans. "No," I answered, and then I beat it out of there.

At school I went past the coaches' office looking to see if Levi was with Hartwell, but it was empty. I kept searching for Levi until I finally spotted him sitting by himself, his head in his hands, out in the courtyard. I was about to go out to talk to him when the warning bell rang.

It was a strange day at school. Kids didn't know whether to congratulate us on making the state tournament or console us because we'd lost so badly to Garfield. We'd sneaked into the state tournament through the back door, and no one liked the feeling.

In Mrs. Miller's English class, we read a story about a man whose wife is perfect except for a single birthmark. The husband gets fixated on the birthmark and makes her try different things to get rid of it. Nothing works, but he can't stop trying new things, and in the end the crazy treatments kill his wife.

As I read that story, I thought about Levi. His situation didn't exactly match, but something was eating at Levi just like that birthmark had eaten at the man. What was it? And why couldn't he tell me about it?

Practice that day was short, just a shoot-around. "Rest," Hartwell said, dismissing us an hour early. "That's the most important thing you can do now."

I knew I could get my mom's car, and we had extra time, so on an impulse after practice I asked Levi if he wanted to go see Mr. Knecht.

"Sure," he said, a spark coming into his eyes.

Knecht's house was in the north end of Seattle, about fifteen minutes from Tangletown. The home itself was small, but his yard was amazing, with curving flower beds, roses on trellises, brick pathways, birdbaths, and fountains. It was winter, so nothing was in bloom, but in summer it must have looked like something out of a garden magazine.

A small greenhouse sat in the back corner. "I bet he's in there," Levi said, and he was right. We found Mr. Knecht at a table pouring dirt into a bunch of little pots. His beard was stubbly, his shirt was misbuttoned, and he had one of those walkers that old people use when a cane doesn't give them enough support. Still, he smiled broadly when he saw us.

We talked basketball for about ten minutes. He asked me if I was the starter, and I said I was. "Fast breaks on every play, right? That was what Hartwell always wanted."

"We fast break a lot," I admitted, "but Hartwell also uses your plays. Actually, he has been using them more and more, especially in the fourth quarter."

Knecht tilted his head. "Are you just saying that to make an old man happy?"

"It's true. Ask Levi."

Knecht looked to Levi, who nodded.

"If it's okay with you, Coach," I said, suddenly understanding why I'd suggested the visit, "I'd like to take a look at what you've done in your yard. We just moved to Seattle, and my mom wants me to fix up our backyard. I need ideas."

It was a weak excuse, but before either of them could object, I was out the door of the greenhouse. Probably Levi wouldn't tell Knecht what was making him so unhappy, but at least he'd have the chance.

I wandered around in Knecht's yard looking at bushes and checking out how he'd set up his compost pile. It was cold, but

I stayed in the yard until the two of them came out—Knecht moving slowly and using his walker—to join me. Knecht shook my hand and thanked me for coming. "I'll try to make it to the championship game, if you get that far," he said, speaking to both of us.

"It'd be great to have you there," I said.

"You're a good kid, Jonas," he answered. "I've followed the team in the newspaper. I'm glad you've gotten your chance; I wasn't doing right by you. I see that now."

His admission froze me for an instant. What could I say? Because he *hadn't* done right by me. "Donny's a good player," I finally managed, "and you knew what he could do."

Knecht frowned. "A good coach keeps his eyes open. Mine were closed."

Back home, I found an envelope from Harding High on the kitchen table—my grades. I ripped it open and there they were—four Bs and two As. I immediately went to Kinko's and faxed a copy to Coach Richter.

Leaving Kinko's, I took a deep breath and exhaled. Richter had my DVD; he had my semester grades; he'd seen my stats as a starter. My push to win a basketball scholarship to Monitor College was coming to an end.

I didn't know that something far more important was just about to begin.

PART FIVE

PART FIVE

1

THE CHEER TEAM STAYED LATE to make posters on Monday night. At school on Tuesday morning, the hallways were decorated with colorful banners screaming GO, HAWKS! and TAKE THE STATE! It was an attempt to wipe out the memory of the Garfield loss, and it worked. "You can do it!" kids called out to me all day.

The brackets had been published in the *Seattle Times*. Garfield was the number one seed—no surprise—and we were a seven seed. That was a huge break for us because it meant that we'd play Garfield again only if we both made it to Saturday night's championship game. There was always the slim chance that some other team would play the game of their lives and knock Garfield out.

Our first game was Thursday in the late afternoon against Lynden High, a school up near the Canadian border. The area is mainly farmland—those guys tend to be football players, not basketball players, or at least that's what Cash told me. They'd lost just once all year, but they hadn't played any big city schools.

All day Tuesday I was impatient to hear from Richter. I'd hoped that my good grades would catch his attention. At lunch and again after school, I used a library computer to check my e-mail.

Nothing.

Tuesday's practice was like Monday's. We walked through our offensive sets, worked a little on a one-three-one trapping zone defense, and finished by going over inbound plays. After we shot free throws, Hartwell blew his whistle and practice was over. "Three games in three nights is a grind," he told us before we left the court. "Sleep well, eat well, keep your mind clear."

If we somehow scratched our way into the finals, I wouldn't have time to do schoolwork, so instead of walking home with Levi, I took my books to the library to get ahead on my reading. It didn't work. I'd read five pages and then stop, and for the next few minutes I'd picture Richter at his desk — my DVD, stat sheets, SAT scores, and grades stacked up on one side, that other kid's stacked up on the other.

After forty-five wasted minutes, I called it quits and headed to Tangletown. My mom had cut back on her hours at work, so she was home that night. We sat together at the kitchen table and ate chicken, mashed potatoes, and corn — none of it microwaved. We were having more and more meals like that.

After dinner I climbed upstairs to my room and checked my e-mail again — more nothing — and then sat at my desk, math book open. Twenty minutes later, my mother called excitedly up the stairs. "Jonas, telephone." As I hurried down the stairs, she whispered what I'd already hoped: "It's Coach Richter."

I picked up the phone. "Hello, this is Jonas."

Coach Richter started by wishing me luck in the upcoming tournament. Then he told me he'd gotten my game films and my semester grades. "I'm impressed with the way you've stepped up these last two months." I don't remember how I replied, but I do remember what he said next. "Buy a heavy coat. New Hampshire is cold in the winter. I'll be putting your scholarship offer into the mail tomorrow morning."

I thanked him twenty times and told him twenty times how hard I'd work both at school and at basketball. I was gripping the telephone as if it were a million-dollar bill.

I'd done it.

Jonas Dolan was going to be a college basketball player.

"One last thing," Coach Richter said. "That forward on your team, the tall quick one — has he got a scholarship lined up?"

"No," I said, excited for Levi. "He doesn't. But he's a great player and a great team guy."

"How is he academically? Is he in college prep classes?"

My heart rate slowed like an Indy car running out of gas. "No, Coach. He's not. It's not that he's stupid or lazy; it's just — I don't know. It's hard to explain."

"I understand. Not everybody is meant for a four-year college right away." Richter paused. "Well, Jonas, you tell your friend that if he enrolls in a junior college and gets decent grades, I'd be interested in bringing him to Monitor College to play for us and with you."

I hung up, and my mother hugged me. "Call your father. Call him right now."

I punched in his number. "That's great!" he screamed through the phone, dishes clattering in the background. "I'm proud of you. In four years, you'll be so smart you'll leave your mom and me in the dust."

"I'm not going to leave anybody in the dust."

"Sure you will, and that's good. We want you to go far; we

always did. We just didn't know how to direct you. I'm glad Coach Russell did. He's the one who got this going, you know. You should call and thank him."

"I will."

"I wish I could buy you a beer to celebrate, but I can't do that, can I?"

I laughed. "No, Dad. I don't think either Coach Richter or Coach Hartwell want me drinking."

"How about this, then? I'll buy you two beers when you graduate from Monitor College."

After we'd talked a couple more minutes, I went back upstairs, feeling excited and itchy, way too itchy to stay in my room. I needed to do something, but what?

Then it hit me. I'd gone through so much with Levi. The hoops at the Good Shepherd Center, the summer games at Green Lake, the frustrating times with Knecht, the turnaround with Hartwell. Levi deserved to be told first, and I had to tell him in person — a phone call just wasn't right.

I grabbed my basketball, walked to his house, and knocked on the door. Rachel, wearing a baggy sweatshirt, answered; her father was peering over her shoulder. She looked at me, her eyes saying: *Thanks.*

"Levi home?"

A minute later he was at the door. "Let's shoot around a little?" I said, motioning with my head for him to come outside.

"Now? It's dark and it's cold."

"It's not that cold, and they put in a floodlight at the Good Shepherd Center. Come on, I've got something important to tell you."

2

EN MINUTES LATER WE WERE playing a lazy one-on-one game in the near dark: no defense, no stellar moves on offense. It was hardly a game at all. "So what's your news?" he asked when I hit a long set shot to win.

"Monitor College. My scholarship came through," I said, grinning in the dark.

Levi was the third person I'd told, but the words — and what they meant — still sounded fantastic to my ear. Was it really true?

He took in what I said, and then he reached out and shook my hand. Not a fist bump or a handclasp; he shook my hand the way adults shake hands. "You deserve it, Jonas."

"There's more," I said, and I told him how much Coach Richter liked his game. "Ask Hartwell to line up a junior college program for you. He'd be glad to do it. You go two years to a junior college, play like you can play, and we could be on the court together in New Hampshire. Wouldn't that be fantastic?"

I expected him to be as excited by the possibility as I was. Instead he lowered his eyes. "Once the tournament is over, I'm finished with Hartwell forever."

That stopped me. Six weeks earlier he'd told me that Hartwell was the smartest man he'd ever known. Why the change? Silence hung in the night air.

"What's wrong with Hartwell?" I finally asked.

Another long pause. And then, when he spoke, Levi's voice was low. "You don't know the truth about him, Jonas. Nobody knows."

My heart rate quickened. "What don't I know?"

The wind rustled the evergreens ringing the court. Clouds moved over the moon.

"What don't I know?" I repeated. The wind moved in the trees again; in the distance, a car sounded its horn. Still he said nothing. "Levi, I'm your friend. What's the point of having a friend if you can't talk to him? It can't be that bad."

"It's worse than anything you can imagine," he said finally, his voice thick with anger. He'd moved back a few steps so that he was almost lost in the dark.

I felt as if I were standing on the edge of a cliff. "Tell me."

I waited, but he stayed silent. So I waited longer. And then, when I was certain he was never going to speak, his words came. "When I'm alone with Hartwell, he asks me to do things."

The world slowed. I felt dizzy, but there was nothing to grab hold of. "What kind of things?"

"On the snow trip to Mount Rainier. That was the first time. And after that at his apartment. He says he's just going to tutor me; that I need his help to stay eligible. And I do need him. I'd have flunked without him and without you. But once we're finished with the schoolwork, he asks me to do things, things he says will help me relax and help him relax. I tell him no, but he talks and talks, and he gets me all confused." Levi paused, and his voice went so soft I could barely hear him. "Sometimes I do them, Jonas. I know they're wrong, but I do them."

I wasn't on the edge of a cliff anymore. I was falling. "Levi, are you talking about sex? Is it sex things he has you do?"

Even though he was deep in the shadows, I could feel him tense. "It's sickening. I'm sickening."

"No, no, Levi. You're not sickening," I said, fighting down panic. "You're not. You needed to tell somebody, and I'm your friend, so you told me. Just let me think about what do, okay? Just let me think for a second."

He stood across from me, his body on alert as if in an instant he might turn and run. Thoughts flashed through my mind with lightning speed. What to do? Go to the principal? Call the police? If I did either, a million spotlights would be on Harding High. *Coach Accused!* That would be the headline. The team would fall apart. Kids at school would want to know: *Who? Who? Who?* Levi's name would come out — things like that always do.

"Listen, Levi," I said, fighting to keep my voice calm. "We'll be done with the state tournament by Saturday night. Let's just play the games out. When our season is over, we can sit down — you and me — and work out a plan, figure out who to tell."

He took a step back. "Jonas, I told you because you're my friend, but I'm not telling anybody else. I'm *never* telling anybody else. Never. My father would kill me if he found out." He paused, and his voice darkened. "I shouldn't have told you. I should never have told you."

I put up my hands to calm him. "No, it's okay. It's okay. You did the right thing. We'll put it aside for a while. There's too much going on right now. Okay?"

"You promise you won't tell anybody?"

"I won't do anything without talking to you first. I promise."

He stepped farther back into the darkness. "I'm going home."

"That sounds good. I'm ready too."

"No. I'm going home alone. I don't want you with me."

"Don't be crazy, Levi. We're heading in the same direction."

"Leave me alone. Just leave me alone."

Before I could answer, he'd turned and raced across the play-field, disappearing into the shadows.

3

IFTEEN MINUTES LATER I WAS in my room, the lights off, my mind and body reeling. I kept trying to come up with some way to make the chaos go away, but Levi had said what he'd said, and there was no going back.

I thought about school, the team, the games. How could I walk the halls of Harding, smile at kids, be a basketball player? How could I even look at Hartwell? Just the thought of him, of what he'd done, made me sick inside.

But when I thought about telling someone — whether it was in a day or a week — that also made me feel sick. Levi's father had screamed at Rachel over a tight blouse; what would he do to Levi? He'd want to kill Hartwell, but he'd blame Levi.

He'd blame his son.

Maybe Levi was right; maybe keeping it secret was the best thing to do. But that would mean Hartwell would get away with what he'd done, and that couldn't happen, because he'd do it again. I'd read about guys like Hartwell in the newspapers. They didn't stop until someone stopped them.

When your mind is buzzing, you think you're going to be awake all night, but you never are. I saw midnight, then one fifteen, then one fifty — but nothing after that. My alarm went off at six, and I sat up with a pounding head and an aching body, as if I'd been in a fight. I slouched downstairs and heated up some milk for hot chocolate and ate a piece of toast.

I left the house at my normal time. I was certain Levi would be gone, but I knocked on his door anyway. His mother answered, her face expressionless. "He left half an hour ago," she said in a monotone, and then she closed the door.

As soon as I stepped inside the school, I started sweating. I'd never felt completely at home in the hallways at Harding, not like I'd felt at home at Redwood High. There were just too many faces I didn't know.

Through my first two classes, I could feel the blood pounding in my head. Luckily, I wasn't called on in either class. When I stepped into Butler's chemistry class, Celia pulled me aside. "Are you okay? Is something wrong?"

"I'm fine," I said, making myself smile. That's when I remembered my scholarship. Celia was the second person at school I'd wanted to tell, after Levi. Now I couldn't bring myself to say a word about Monitor College. Had Richter called me just last night? It seemed years ago.

As the day dragged on, a new dread came on: practice. Seeing Levi and Hartwell together would make everything more real and more horrible. How could I look at either of them? Winning or losing didn't matter. Basketball didn't matter. All I wanted was for everything and everyone to go away.

As I was standing at my locker right before health class, I spotted Hartwell in a side hallway. The instant I saw his face, the ground beneath me moved. My heart started pounding fast, the blood rushed into my head, but then it was as if all the blood had gone out of me. I was burning up, and a second later I was chilled. I felt the dizziness come, felt myself start to fall, but someone's hands reached out and grabbed me and held me upright. It was Gokul. "Are you all right?" he asked.

"I don't know," I said.

He helped me to the nurse's office, where Mrs. Van Deusen had me lie down on a cot. She stuck a thermometer into my mouth, and her eyes went to her watch. "I'm fine," I said when Mrs. Van Deusen took the thermometer out.

She scowled. "You're not fine. You've got a fever of one hundred and one. I'm calling your mother; you need to go home." She looked to Gokul, who had stayed. "You can go back to class now."

Gokul was about to leave when I remembered practice.

"Can you tell somebody on the team that I'm going home sick?"

"Yeah, sure," Gokul said. "Cash is in my sixth-period class. I'll tell him."

"Thanks."

Gokul patted me on the shoulder, a smile on his face. "You get healthy, Jonas. Everybody knows we've got no chance to win the whole thing. But we've really got no chance without you."

My mother arrived twenty minutes later. Once I was home, I went up to my room and tried to read *Sports Illustrated,* but the words swam on the page and the dizziness wouldn't go away. I gave up, flicked off the light, and fell asleep.

I didn't wake up until ten o'clock the next morning.

When I saw how late it was, I jumped out of bed, dressed quickly, and rushed downstairs. My mother and father were both at the kitchen drinking coffee. "Why didn't you wake me?" I said.

"You needed to sleep," my mother said.

"But —"

My dad spoke next. "Jonas, I talked to Coach Hartwell. He says you have to be at school for your afternoon classes or you can't play against Lynden, but that you can rest until then. You've got a couple more hours. Take it easy — you're going to need your energy."

4

THE DIZZINESS WASN'T COMPLETELY GONE, but at least I didn't feel as if my knees were made of Jell-O anymore. I ate lunch at home, and then my mother drove me to Harding. As I got out of the car, I forced myself to stand tall. I could do this; I could get through the state tournament and then face whatever would come after.

Spanish class was Spanish class. I answered a few questions, read a little about Picasso, and the hour went by. It was health that I dreaded — Levi would be there.

I lingered in the hallway until just before the bell rang. I knew where Levi was without even looking. All year I'd taken the seat next to him in the back row. But I couldn't sit next to Levi and pretend that everything was okay, so I used my tardiness as an excuse to take an open desk toward the front. A couple of times during class I looked back toward him, but both times his head was down. He didn't want to see me, either.

When class ended, I waited for him by the door. It would have looked strange if we'd gone to the team bus separately, and I think he sensed that too. As we walked to the parking lot, kids called out, wishing us luck.

There were about fifty kids in the parking lot. Some of the guys were already on the bus, and they shouted out the window to their friends, who shouted encouragement back. I didn't join in, and neither did Levi. He grabbed a seat up front, next to Brandon, so I headed to the back.

We'd been on the bus for five minutes before Hartwell climbed on. He stopped all the screaming with a look. "Wait until you've won something before you celebrate."

The guys stayed quiet as Hartwell gave a short lecture on keeping our focus. As I watched him, the unreality of it returned. Hartwell was so classy — tall, lean but strong, well dressed. He had a ready smile and always knew what to say. And he had just the right amount of swagger in everything he did. If someone had asked me two days earlier: *Who do you want to be like when you're twenty-five?* I'd have answered: *Ryan Hartwell.*

I looked at Levi. His eyes were fixed on the floor. What sort of hell was he going through? I felt a new surge of white-hot hatred for Hartwell, for that classy look, for that easy manner, and for that arrogance. He'd searched out a target, like a hawk circling over a field. He'd found Levi, and he'd struck.

Hartwell finished his talk and then said something to the bus driver. I closed my eyes as we pulled out of the parking lot. In front of me guys talked, but nobody was loud. Somewhere during the hourlong ride, I went into a semi-trance, doing everything I could to turn my mind off.

I came out of it when the bus exited the freeway. The sound of the motor changed; the speed of the bus changed, and the Tacoma Dome was right there, an American flag waving from the top of the blue and white roof.

We pulled to a stop in the parking lot. I grabbed my duffle bag, stood, and was immediately overwhelmed again by the sense that the earth was quaking beneath me. I was so lightheaded that I had to grab hold of the back of the seat to keep from falling. Somehow I managed to make my way off the bus and follow Hartwell through the players' entrance into the locker room.

I sat down on a bench, my head still swimming, and changed into my uniform. When everybody was ready, Hartwell called us together and gave us a final pep talk. I don't know what he said: I was too afraid I wouldn't be able to walk to pay attention. It was as if I were on the deck of a tiny sailboat in the middle of a typhoon.

Around me, guys hollered things like, "Let's win this thing!" and "This is our time!" Moments later they stood and ran out of the locker room and through the tunnel. Seconds earlier I didn't think I could walk, but somehow I was swept up and out with them.

And then an amazing thing happened. As soon as I stepped onto the basketball court, the world steadied. I looked at Levi, and I could see relief wash over his face too. "Just play," I mouthed to him, and he nodded.

We were where we belonged.

We went through the lay-up line a couple of times and shot around for a few minutes. There were photographers and TV cameramen everywhere — the game was going to be broadcast live across the state. When our warm-ups ended, the lights went dim. One by one, the starters for both teams were introduced, while multicolored searchlights cut the darkness and rock music blared from the speakers.

None of the fanfare mattered; none of it made me nervous. On the basketball court, the rules were clear; the goal was clear. Hartwell was no longer a person: he was a coach, and I could listen to the coach, even though I hated the man. On the basketball court, I was safe.

The full lights came back on, and the horn sounded.

It was game time.

As I walked to center court, I sized up the opposition. Lynden High was starting four white guys and a Hispanic guy. Not one of them was very tall, crazy muscular, or amazingly athletic. They were just guys.

Levi directed the opening tip to Cash, who corralled the ball and passed it to me. I brought it to the top of the key, and Cash used a screen by Nick to pop free in the corner. I hit him with a perfect pass, and he stepped into a high-arcing three-pointer.

Swish!

Cash's gorgeous shot made a jittery Lynden team even more jittery. On their first possession, Lynden's forward fumbled a pass out-of-bounds. Cash hustled the ball inbounds; I raced into the forecourt and fed Levi, who was set up on the low block. The guy guarding me dropped down to double-team; Levi kicked the ball right back to me; and I drained a wide-open three-pointer. After another Lynden turnover, Levi grabbed an offensive rebound and stuffed the put-back, giving us an 8–0 lead fifty-two seconds into the game. The Lynden coach jumped off the bench to call time-out.

Lynden's time-out worked . . . sort of. After our red-hot start, the game settled down. They were a solid team; they wouldn't have made it into the state quarterfinals if they weren't. We didn't score on dunks and three-pointers every time down; and they didn't fumble the ball away on every possession.

Even though Lynden played better than they had at the beginning of the game, and even though we had our cold spells, we were never threatened. All four quarters, I let the game come to me. On offense, my passes were crisp, my decisions solid. On defense, I clogged the passing lanes and rotated when I was needed. I never looked at the score or the clock. I was totally in the moment, and Levi was there with me. He hauled down rebounds, blocked shots, scored on put-backs and power moves. When the horn finally sounded ending the game, cheers rolled down on us from the stands. I looked up at the scoreboard: Harding, 68; Lynden, 48.

It should have been a moment of pure elation. I should have luxuriated in the cheers washing over me. But Hartwell had stolen any joy. I hated the cheers because they meant the game was over. I wanted to stay on the court and play and play and play. I wanted to play a thousand games, one after the other.

5

ONZAGA PREP WAS PLAYING BELLARMINE in the next game, and we'd play the winner the following night. Hartwell was staying to scout the game, which meant the bus was staying. "If you've got a ride home, and you want to leave, it's okay with me. If you want to stay and watch, that's also okay. Those of you that leave — don't celebrate too much, because we've got another game in twenty-four hours."

Most of the guys stayed, but I asked Levi if he wanted a ride home, and he nodded. We met my parents outside the locker room.

On the drive back to Seattle, my mom and dad were talkative at first, telling both Levi and me how great we'd played. You can only do that for so long, though, so soon we all lapsed into silence. My parents were worn out from cheering; we were worn out from playing. Still, I was glad my parents were there — it made it impossible for us to talk about Hartwell. The ride to the T-Dome had seemed to take ten hours; the ride back felt like it was over in ten minutes.

My dad dropped Levi off; Levi didn't even look at me as he got of the car. Back home, I ate a microwaved burrito and followed that with a bowl of chocolate ice cream. My mom sat across from me, but we didn't talk much. When the ice cream was gone, I retreated to my room, where I checked my text messages and my e-mails. Coach Richter had sent congratulations, and so had Celia and Uncle Frank.

I answered them all and then remembered that the Gonzaga-Bellarmine game was on a local television station. I went downstairs and flicked it on — Gonzaga led by eight with five minutes to play. I didn't turn the TV off until the Gonzaga guys were jumping around at center court, celebrating. When I did flick it off, I felt completely exhausted. That was good — it meant I'd be able to sleep. And I did, until three thirty. After that I tossed and turned, wanting the night to end, but not wanting the next day to begin.

I stopped by Levi's house on Friday morning, but he'd already left for school — no surprise — so I walked alone to Harding High. As soon as I stepped inside, I felt the hallways buzzing with excitement. Our victory over Lynden had electrified the students and the faculty. Even kids who never followed sports smiled at me, slapped me on the back, and wished me luck.

There was a pep rally last period. The school band played the fight song; Hartwell talked about sportsmanship and effort; Mr. Diaz again lectured everyone about driving safely. "This is a great time for Harding High. Don't ruin it by killing yourself or someone else."

When the pep rally ended, the team headed to the parking lot, where the bus waited to take us to the Tacoma Dome. Levi got on before me and hunkered down by himself in the back, so I took a seat up front.

After the locker room and Hartwell's pregame instructions, I kept waiting for the adrenaline rush, but it didn't come. I didn't really want to be there, but where else did I want to be? As I laced up my shoes, I imagined myself at Monitor College, far away from Hartwell both in space and time. I'd have new teammates and a new coach. I'd be playing in a new state, separated from everything familiar. I'd always been slightly afraid of that moment, but now I *wanted* to get away. To get away and have Hartwell and Harding High behind me. To have Levi behind me, too.

Finally it was time for Cash and me to lead the team onto the court. It was a win-or-go-home game, but the hair on my arms didn't stand up; my spine didn't tingle. The energy, the focus, the desire — they weren't there. Still, I was a leader of the team; I had to dig deep and *find* the energy, the focus, the desire. I had to suck it up and face everything — the basketball games and then what would come afterward . . . what had to come afterward.

6

AS HOT AS WE WERE at the start of the game against Lynden, that's how cold we were against Gonzaga. On our first possession, Cash crossed over on his guy, drove into the lane, and smacked into a defender who'd rotated over to draw the charge. No big deal, except Cash did exactly the same thing on our next possession, with the same result. One minute into the game, our top scorer was sitting on the bench in foul trouble.

Early in the season, when Cash had been our only true scoring threat, we would have been beaten. Nick, DeShawn, even Levi — none of them had trusted their own ability, especially on the offensive end of the court. Now we were a complete team. I sized up Gonzaga's defense, looking for a mismatch, and found one. The guy guarding Levi was huge but slow — he couldn't handle Levi one-on-one.

I set up a two-man game to see how Gonzaga would defend. As soon as I dumped the ball into Levi, my guy left me and dropped down to harass Levi. That meant they knew they couldn't cover him straight up. Once the double-team came, Levi passed the ball back to me. I was wide open for a three-pointer, but I missed long. A couple possessions later, we ran the same play and again I missed the wide-open shot.

I wasn't the only one off target. We couldn't hit the ocean with a rock, while everything Gonzaga tossed up seemed to go in. A couple of minutes into the game, we were down six, and for a third time I missed a wide-open shot, this time short. Hartwell yelled something at me, but as I backpedaled to play defense, DeShawn gave me a thumbs-up. "Keep shooting," he shouted. From the bench I heard Cash yell the same thing.

That support gave me the boost I needed. The next time we worked the play, my release was free and easy. The ball hit the back of the rim and went down. A minute later, I hit another long three-pointer, cutting Gonzaga's lead to four points.

Those two outside shots opened up the inside for Levi. Gonzaga couldn't run the double-team at him because they had to cover me, and their big lug couldn't handle Levi's speed one-on-one. All through the second quarter, Levi took that hulk to the hoop, either making baskets or passing to DeShawn whenever DeShawn's guy rotated over to help. As those two piled up points, we inched into the lead.

We couldn't put Gonzaga away, though. The big guy who couldn't guard Levi? On the other end, Levi couldn't guard him. He'd post up down low, they'd feed him the ball, and he'd muscle up short jumpers and baby hooks. For a huge guy — he must have weighed 260 — he had a soft touch. None of their other players were great, but they knocked down a decent percentage of shots, and they didn't turn the ball over.

Early in the third quarter, Gonzaga hit back-to-back three-pointers to retake the lead. Hartwell called time and used it to put Cash, who'd sat out the entire second quarter, into the game. Rested and ready, he hit a midrange jump shot to tie the game and then circled back to steal the inbound pass, made the lay-up, and was fouled. After he sank the free throw, our lead was three points.

We used Cash's hot hand to slowly push our lead to twelve late in the quarter. As the final seconds of the game ticked away, I looked at the scoreboard and realized we'd done it. We'd won a game when we weren't playing our best — any of us. We'd won it on mental toughness. Gonzaga, like Lynden, was dead. There was just one team left to beat: Garfield.

We were in the finals.

7

I WAS DOG-TIRED AFTER THE GAME. My head hurt. I wanted to go home with my parents, but Hartwell insisted that the whole team stay to watch the Garfield game. "These guys aren't as good as you think," he said. "You watch them closely, and you'll know you can beat them."

We sat together as a team on the second level. I found a spot as far from Hartwell as possible, but before the tip-off he called me over to him. "I want you to hear what I've got to say about the individual players. It'll help you tomorrow."

My body broke into a sweat. In the locker room before the game, during time-outs, at halftime — at those times I was able to block out everything except basketball. But the Hartwell who joked with the fans around him, the Hartwell who ate a hot dog and drank a Coke and cracked peanut shells in his teeth — that Hartwell wasn't a coach. That Hartwell was the man who'd done those things to Levi.

I sat at his elbow — my jaw clenched, my stomach in knots — and listened as he analyzed Garfield's strengths and weaknesses. He saw so much; he knew so much. But his knowledge of the game made everything worse. He'd been more than a coach to me; he'd been like an older brother, a person I'd trusted completely.

On the ride back to Seattle, I sat alone in a seat in the middle of the bus. When we were about ten miles from Harding High, I moved back next to Levi. I didn't say anything for a while, but after a few minutes I spoke, my voice hushed so that no one else could hear. "You doing okay?"

"Yeah, I'm doing okay."

"I mean with Hartwell? You managing okay?"

"I don't see him anymore."

"What do you mean?"

"Just what I said. I look at him, but I don't see him."

I nodded, even though I only half understood. "Listen, Levi. Here's what we'll do. We'll play it out tomorrow—you and me. That's how we started, remember? Back in the summer—you and me. Once the title game is over, then we'll get help—you and me. We'll go to the principal or a counselor or whoever you want. It'll be your choice, but I'll be with you every step of the way. I promise. Okay?"

He looked out the window. "No, it's not okay."

"What's not okay?"

"I'm not going to anybody about this. I keep telling you that, but you won't listen to me. What happened with Hartwell is over—nothing like that is ever going to happen again, so nobody has to know. Just keep your mouth shut."

Right then Hartwell turned in his seat and looked back at us. I quickly looked out the window. "Levi," I whispered, once Hartwell had again faced forward, "he'll look for somebody else; you know he will."

He shook his head. "I don't know that, and neither do you. Not for sure you don't. So forget I ever told you anything. Just wipe it out of your mind. Go to that college and forget you ever knew me."

With that, he got up and moved to a seat toward the front of the bus. I stared out the window, thinking back to the night I'd heard about my scholarship, the night we'd gone to the Good Shepherd Center and what he'd told me there.

I wished that I could do what Levi wanted. With every atom in my body, I wished that I could erase those five minutes from my memory. But how could I ever wipe that night out of my mind? I should have told somebody right away. I don't know why I didn't — fear maybe, or shock, or because Levi didn't want me to, or maybe because I didn't want to blow up the season. For whatever reason, I'd chosen not to do anything.

Now I'd play out the season and then speak with Levi one final time. If he wouldn't go with me to the principal, then I'd go alone. Mr. Diaz would call the police, and they'd question Levi. Once that happened, the truth would come out. Because Levi wouldn't lie. Once someone asked him what had happened, he'd tell the truth.

That's who he was.

8

LEVI'S PICTURE WAS ON THE front page of the sports section of Saturday's *Seattle Times*. The photo was tucked away in the bottom right corner, but it was on the front page. The headline read:

LEVI RAWDON LEADS HARDING HAWKS INTO FINAL

The story talked about how he'd come on strong as the year had progressed, emerging from nowhere to become a star. I read the article twice, both times knowing he'd be embarrassed, but hoping that he'd also feel good about himself.

I ate breakfast and then prowled around all morning, watching TV, playing video games, flipping through magazines. The nerves started around noon; I had to force myself to eat lunch. After that I watched more TV and played more video games. It was as if the minutes and hours were stuck in mud.

At last it was time to head to the parking lot to get on the team bus for the final ride to Tacoma. I checked my duffle bag to make certain my uniform was packed, and then my dad drove me to

Harding High. "Whether you win or lose doesn't matter," he said as he pulled into the lot. "The way you've hung in there, the character you've shown — that's what matters."

I felt my throat tighten. He knew only what I'd done in the light of day; he didn't know about the things I'd kept hidden. I managed to thank him, though my voice was shaky. I climbed out of the car and then leaned back in. "After the game, Coach Hartwell wants the whole team to go back on the bus together. So I won't be needing a ride back from the T-Dome."

He nodded. "Your mom and I will meet you right here then, in the parking lot."

"You don't have to. I can walk home."

"State champions don't walk home." He smiled. "And neither do runners-up."

After he drove off, I walked to the bus, threw my duffle bag into the loading bay, and climbed on board. Cash was in a front seat, holding the *Seattle Times*. "Did you see this?" he said, pointing to the article about Levi. "I'm going to razz him bigtime. The writer has Levi confused with LeBron James." DeShawn and Nick were nearby, both of them grinning at the prospect of needling Levi.

I looked across the parking lot and spotted Levi heading toward the bus. "Don't do it," I said.

"What are you talking about?" Cash snapped. "I'd just be kidding him."

"You know Levi. If you want him to play well, don't razz him. He's not the kind of guy you can razz."

For a second I thought Cash would ignore me, but then his eyes showed that he understood. "Yeah, yeah, yeah, Jonas. You're right. We'll lay off him. But at least we can tell him that we read the article."

"Sure," I said. "It would be weird if you didn't."

When Levi got on the bus a few minutes later, Cash and the other guys surrounded him, newspaper in hand. Cash pointed to the newspaper and said something I didn't hear. Levi's face reddened, and then Cash whacked him a couple of times on the back and shook his arm, smiling the whole time. Levi smiled back— a big, wide smile. Then Hartwell climbed on board, and Levi's smile disappeared in a blink. Hartwell told everyone to sit down and did a quick head count. The door hissed shut, and the bus headed to the Tacoma Dome.

9

B Y THE TIME WE WERE in uniform and ready to take the floor, the guys were like guitar strings wound so tightly that they were ready to snap. I was wound up too, but beneath the excitement I felt strangely calm.

Hartwell must have given us a pep talk in the locker room, though I don't remember a word. We took the court and went through our normal pregame routines, only nothing felt normal about them. Everything — the noise, the crowd, the cameras — had been ratcheted up ten notches. It was like being in the center of a tornado; familiar things were all around, but they were flying by so fast that they were hard to recognize.

Just before game time, Coach Knecht wobbled across the court to join the team. He was using a cane and had a man — maybe his son — at his elbow. The Harding fans stood for Knecht, stamping their feet and roaring. The cheering was so loud that the Garfield guys stopped their warm-ups to watch. Coach Knecht waved to the crowd. Hartwell, all smiles, motioned for Knecht to sit next to him, but Knecht tottered to the end of our bench, taking a seat next to Brandon, who hadn't played in three weeks.

The Garfield guys came out playing fast, trying to knock us

out in the first minutes of the game by intimidating us with their speed and power. But the line between *fast* and *too fast* is thin, and they crossed it.

The calm I felt had stayed with me despite the roaring crowd, so I used Garfield's aggression against them. They went for my fakes, trying for steals, and in the first five minutes, Cash and Levi beat them three times for backdoor lay-ins.

We also caught some breaks from the refs. They knew about the scuffle in our last Garfield game, and they were not going to let the state championship game turn into a street brawl. That worked against Garfield, because this time around when they muscled Levi, they were whistled for fouls. When the buzzer sounded ending the first quarter, we were up, 12–10.

We had a decent numbers of supporters, though fewer than Garfield, but there were a couple of thousand people in the stands who were just basketball fans. They'd come in expecting to see Garfield run us out of the gym. Instead, the game had taken on a David-and-Goliath feel, with us playing the role of David. Most of those people came over to our side, hoping to see Goliath go down. Having the crowd on your side is a big deal in a championship game. Most experts say crowd noise is worth at least six points, and some say it's worth as many as ten.

During the break at the end of the quarter, I studied the faces of the Garfield guys. Their jaws were clenched, but there was doubt in their eyes. The longer we hung with them, the tighter they'd get. We didn't have to be in the lead, but we had to stay close. If they ever pulled ahead by ten, then they'd relax and their talent could easily push the lead out to twenty.

Throughout the second and third quarters, we used the best

parts of Hartwell's style and Knecht's — fast breaking when we had an advantage, working the shot clock when we didn't. We stayed out of foul trouble, didn't turn the ball over much, shot a decent percentage. The Garfield guys made the sensational plays, but every basket counts the same — sensational or ordinary. They were better than we were, but we were more in sync, and I was the director, setting up each play.

At the end of the third quarter, we led, 41–40.

10

I N THE FOURTH QUARTER, the game completely changed. On their first possession, a Garfield player came flying down the lane. He soared in the air for the lay-up, knocking me flat on my back on his way to the hoop. I looked to the ref, wondering if he'd call a charge or a block. To my astonishment, he called nothing. And that's how it went. The refs had held a tight rein for three quarters, but they didn't want to determine the final outcome, so in the fourth quarter they swallowed their whistles and let us play.

I struggled to adjust. More than once after I got knocked to the ground, I growled at the ref for not calling anything. And the Garfield guys went after Levi even more than they went after me. My frustration kept growing by the minute.

About midway through the quarter, Hartwell called a timeout. He used it to complain about a non-call on a slashing drive to the hoop by Cash. While Hartwell was arguing with the officials, Coach Knecht motioned for me to come down to him. When I was a couple feet away from him, he grabbed me by the elbow and yanked me to him. "Stop begging for calls," he shouted at me, gripping my arm so tightly it hurt. "No one is going to give you a championship. Get out there and take it." There was elation in his voice.

Hartwell had finished complaining to the refs and was madly motioning for me to join the huddle. Knecht let go of my arm, and I hurried to join my teammates. Hartwell yelled something I couldn't hear just as the horn sounded, calling us back to the court.

The final four minutes of the game were a war. Cash muscled up a jump shot, banking it in off the glass; Garfield answered with a put-back down low, the Garfield guy grunting like an animal after stuffing the ball through. Back and forth, up and down the court, one play after another. The T-Dome was electric loud; you could feel the place sweat. I heard the roars of the crowd, but somehow I didn't hear them — or at least they didn't affect me. With just over a minute left, I crossed over on my guy, went up and under, scored the hoop, and was fouled so hard I ended up flat on my back. Even then there was no whistle, so I scrambled to my feet and ran back to play defense, peeking at the scoreboard as I did.

Garfield ran a set play, isolating their guard against me down low. He bumped me and bumped me, working closer and closer to the hoop. *I'm going to stop you; I'm going to stop you.* That's what I thought, but just when I was certain he was going to spin right, he stepped back and swished a jump shot over me.

Game tied.

Twenty-two seconds remaining. Everyone in the gym was up, screaming. I brought the ball into forecourt and passed it to De-Shawn. He looked shocked to get it and passed it right back to me as if it were on fire. I worked my way to the top of the key, keeping my dribble alive. If nothing opened, I'd drive to the hoop.

That's when I spotted Cash down low, setting a back screen for Levi. Ten seconds were left in the game. Levi faked like he was coming to right wing and then broke to the hoop. I flipped the ball up toward the backboard. Levi rose into the air and — in one motion — caught it and slammed it down.

The place erupted.

Could it really happen?

Could Harding really beat Garfield?

Garfield's coach immediately signaled for a time-out. While we huddled around Hartwell, the refs checked the television monitor and put four seconds on the clock.

The horn sounded and both teams returned to the court. This was it — the final play. Levi was jumping up and down trying to distract Garfield's inbound passer, but he still managed to heave the ball two-thirds of the way downcourt. I tipped it, the ball bounced once, and then a Garfield guy grabbed it and in one motion flung the ball toward the hoop. The horn sounded while the ball was in the air. My heart sank: I was sure it was going to be one of those shots that end up on YouTube, a miracle game-winner that would be seen by millions.

Instead, the ball missed the backboard entirely, ending up in the lap of a man sitting four rows up. A couple of Garfield guys fell to their knees and then dropped to their elbows, heads down. I caught Levi's eye, and we just stared at each other for a long moment.

We'd done it.

A second later, Cash grabbed me from behind and swung me toward center court. Suddenly all the guys were there, and we jumped around for a while, a crazed mob, all of us as one. Every once in a while, I peeked back up at the scoreboard. The numbers didn't change. We'd beaten Garfield.

We were state champions.

11

THE TROPHY CEREMONY AT CENTER court was chaotic. Photographers shoved cameras into my face as I shook hands with a bunch of people I didn't know, most of whom said things I couldn't hear. Somebody from the state Athletic Association handed a trophy to Hartwell, and then Hartwell handed it to Coach Knecht. Knecht tried to hand it back to Hartwell, and finally the two of them together raised it up into the air. The Harding fans who had hung around cheered wildly, and they cheered again when Levi was named MVP of the tournament. A man from the state Athletic Association gave a short speech, and then somebody from the Dairy Farmers Association thanked a whole bunch of people, and at last the ceremony was over.

Back in the locker room, Hartwell told us that he'd arranged a pizza party for us in Seattle. "You can phone your girlfriends and parents, but we can't have the whole school. Okay?"

For the first few minutes, we were loud in the locker room, but we were too exhausted to keep the high going. I was glad to climb on the bus; a long ride back in the dark was just what I wanted.

I sat next to Levi. I had him pull the MVP trophy out of his duffle bag so I could look at it. "You deserved this," I said. "You were great in every single game."

He took the trophy back from me and zipped it up again.

"You could go to Shoreline Community College next year," I said in an excited whisper. "I looked it up; they've always got good teams. You could play for them for a couple of years, and then transfer to UW or someplace like that. You're way better than me, you know."

Levi shook his head. "Come on, Jonas. What would I study in college?"

"You could be an art major, for one thing, with the way you draw. Or you could study forestry or something like that. I don't know what I'm going to study, but I'm going."

"You can study the forest in college?"

"They have forestry classes at Monitor College. If Monitor has them, then UW would have them too."

"You really think I could go to college?"

"Yes, I do."

There was a long pause. The lights of Tacoma were behind us; we'd entered a dark stretch of freeway. "You're not going to let it drop, are you?" Levi said, his voice low.

My mouth went dry. I swallowed. "I've told you. I can't. And I've told you why. But I'll be with you every step of the way. We'll do this together."

He turned away from me and looked out the window; I closed my eyes and let the time pass. There was nothing left to say.

When we pulled into the Harding High parking lot, about fifty people were waiting for us, and they cheered when we stepped off the bus. My dad hugged me and told me how proud he was. My mom kissed me before giving me the keys to the Subaru. I told her that parents were invited to the party, but she shook her head. "It's for you and your teammates, not for us. Enjoy yourself."

I drove with Levi to Zeeks Pizza on Phinney Avenue. "Let's forget about everything and just have a good time tonight," I said.

He nodded. "Sure, Jonas. Whatever you say."

After I'd parked the Subaru, I realized my sweats didn't have any pockets, so I shoved the keys under the floor mat and left the doors unlocked.

Before we'd gotten on the bus, Cash and some of the other guys had texted their girlfriends about the party. I'd texted Celia, though I didn't think she'd show. But as I got out of the car, I saw her across the parking lot. She waved to me and smiled, and I walked quickly over to where she stood.

As I neared her, she reached out and hugged me. "That was so exciting, Jonas! Congratulations!"

I smiled. "Thanks for coming."

"Thanks for asking me."

And then we stood, neither of us knowing what to do.

"Are you hungry?" I asked at last.

"Not as hungry as you must be, but I could eat."

We went inside. The back table was filled with bowls of salad, bread sticks, soft drinks, and six different kinds of pizza.

We ate and talked, and then around eleven Cash started dancing with his girlfriend in a little room off to the side, and soon other kids joined in. Rachel, who was wearing a skintight, low-cut top, danced with DeShawn.

"Do you feel like dancing?" I asked Celia.

She shook her head. "Let's just talk."

So that's what we did. About Central Washington University and about Monitor College. I'd been focused on Levi and basketball for so long that it felt good to think about something else.

At twelve forty-five, Hartwell stopped the music to tell us that Zeeks was closing. "Make sure you get all your stuff before you leave, and if you want any more pizza, get it now."

Hartwell's voice snapped me out of the calm place where I'd been. Things needed to be done, and soon. I looked around for Levi and Rachel, figuring I'd give them both a ride home. I couldn't find Levi, but Rachel was about ten feet away, pulling a sweatshirt over her head.

Celia and I walked over to her. "Have you seen Levi?" I asked.

Rachel shook her head. "He's probably outside. He's supposed to walk me home."

"I can give you both a ride, if you want."

The three of us headed out to the parking lot. It had turned cold and rainy, and the wind had come up. I scanned the area looking for Levi but didn't find him. I thought it was possible he'd gone home earlier, but not likely. He'd have said something to Rachel before he left. I looked over to where my mom's Subaru was parked and then looked again.

It wasn't there.

For a second I thought I must have parked it someplace else, even though I knew I hadn't. My eyes searched every corner of the parking lot. No Subaru.

"What's wrong?" Rachel asked, hugging herself to keep warm.

"My mom's car is gone. I parked it right there, and now it's gone."

The three of us stared at the empty parking spot as if the car might magically reappear.

"Do you think somebody stole it?" Celia asked.

"I don't know. Maybe. I left the keys under the mat."

Rachel spun around to face me. "Did Levi know about the keys?"

"Yeah. He saw me put them there. Why?"

"Maybe he stole it," Rachel said.

"Come on," I said, the cold biting at me. "Your brother? Stealing a car?"

Rachel's eyes scanned the lot. "He's gone, right? And your car's gone. I mean . . . What else?"

I felt my body sag. Was Rachel right?

"Try his cell phone," Celia suggested. "There's got to be some explanation."

"He doesn't have one."

"He stole your car," Rachel said, a smile of disbelief on her face. "My brother stole your car."

Celia gave Rachel and me a ride to Tangletown. As she drove, the only sound was the car heater going full blast. When we neared my house, I peered out into the darkness, hoping I'd see the Subaru parked either in front of Levi's house or my own, but it wasn't there. "Is there anything I can do?" Celia asked as she pulled up in front of Levi's house.

"No, but don't worry. There's got to be some simple explanation."

Rachel and I climbed out of the car and headed up the walkway to Rachel's house. Her father was waiting in the front room.

"Is Levi here?" Rachel asked as soon as she opened the door.

"No," her father said, walking toward her. "He's supposed to be with you, making sure you're safe."

"Then he's out drinking," she said, her eyes burning with a strange excitement. "He stole Jonas's car, and he's out drinking."

"What is she talking about?" her father said, looking at me.

I stepped into the warm house and closed the door behind me. Her dad listened to my story, and then had me repeat the whole thing. "You should call the police," he said firmly after I finished the second time.

"I don't want to do that, Mr. Rawdon. Even if he took the Subaru, he didn't really steal it. We're friends and all. He just borrowed it."

"He stole it," Rachel said. Then she wheeled on her father. "You always thought he was perfect, and I was just a tramp. Well, he stole a car and got drunk, and he's probably got some slutty girl with him too. So what do you think of him now?"

"Go to your room," her father commanded. She glared at him for a moment and then disappeared down the hallway.

The two of us stood facing each other. Finally he spoke. "If Levi is drinking alcohol with a girl, then the proper thing is to report your car as stolen. He needs to be arrested before anyone is hurt."

"Mr. Rawdon, he's not drinking. Not Levi. You know he's not. And he's not with a girl, either."

He stood, still and silent, for a long time. "Then what is he doing, Jonas?"

12

HURRIED HOME — THE RAIN had stopped, but it was bitter cold — and opened the door to a dark, quiet house. I was glad my parents hadn't waited up for me. I slipped upstairs, took a shower, and then lay down on my bed, trying to make sense of what had happened. Every time a car drove by, I jumped up hoping to see the Subaru.

Around two I fell asleep, but I was awake again at four. I got out of bed and went downstairs and out into the street. The rain had stopped, but it was freezing out; it almost felt as if it might snow. I walked to Levi's house, hoping to see the car in his driveway. Nothing. I did the same thing again at six. I was sound asleep at seven thirty when my dad shook me awake. "Jonas, are you okay? Were you in an accident?"

"No, no. I'm fine."

"So where's your mom's car?"

Ten minutes later, my dad was angrily punching numbers into the telephone. "Who are you calling?" I asked.

"The police. Which is what you should have done last night."

"He's not drinking, Dad."

"Fine, Jonas. I believe you. But he's in some kind of trouble. Once I report the Subaru as stolen, the police will look for him."

An hour later I told my story again, this time to a Detective Wanda Brockman, a large black policewoman who took notes as she fired questions at me.

"We've got no reports of any accidents anywhere in Puget Sound involving a Subaru," she said, when the questions ended. She was looking at my dad and mom and totally ignoring me. "My guess is that the boy is probably passed out on the side of some road somewhere."

"You don't know Levi," I said, heatedly. "There's no way he's drunk."

She looked at me, and her eyebrows went up. "And you don't know how many times I've heard that." She sighed. "Give me his address. I need to talk to his parents."

I told her the house number. "It's down the street. Should I come?"

She shook her head. "No, you stay here. This is my job, not yours."

When she left, my mom looked hard at me. "Is something going on with Levi? Some problem that might make him pack up and leave?"

I stiffened. "No."

She stared at me. "Jonas, are you keeping something back? Some secret? Because if you are —"

"There's nothing." As I spoke, I forced myself to look her in the eye, even though every part of me wanted to look away.

⊛ ⊛ ⊛

The hours crawled by. I kept looking out the window, hoping to see Levi pull up in front of the house. I ate lunch before calling Celia. "Have you told anybody about the car and Levi?"

"No. Is he back?"

"Not yet. Listen, don't tell anyone, okay?"

"I wouldn't do that," she said.

"I'm sorry. I'm just . . . I don't know."

After I hung up, I grabbed my basketball and headed to the Good Shepherd Center. I didn't feel like shooting around, but I was too nervous to stay in the house, and I couldn't think of anything else to do.

As I tossed up shots, my mind burned with questions. *Where was Levi? What was he doing? When was he coming back? Was he coming back?* I had no answers, but I knew what was behind it all. Levi was gone because he knew I'd make him talk about Hartwell.

I trudged home, ate some dinner, went upstairs, closed my door, turned off the light, and just lay on my bed, wanting time to pass. Around seven thirty I heard a knock on the door. I hurried downstairs to see Rachel stepping into our living room. My mother motioned for Rachel to sit on the sofa, and then she left us alone. I sat next to Rachel, and she took from her purse a sheet of paper that had Levi's picture at the top with the word MISSING underneath.

"My mom and dad want me to make fifty copies and put them up around the neighborhood. I was hoping maybe you would help."

"When are you putting them up?"

"Now, I guess."

"I think we should wait a little longer, at least until tomorrow. I have a gut feeling that he'll be back soon."

"Okay." She paused. "I didn't mean what I said about him drinking and being with a girl."

"I know you didn't."

Her head dropped; her voice got small. "Jonas, I'm scared. What if something terrible has happened?"

"Nothing terrible has happened," I said, and then I hugged her the way I'd seen Levi hug his little sisters.

After Rachel left, I dragged myself back upstairs to my dark room. Once she posted those flyers, word would be everywhere. There'd be an article in the newspaper. *MVP DISAPPEARS!* Everyone would think Levi was crazy or a thief or both. He had to come back, and soon.

And then, suddenly, I knew where he was.

I fumbled through my wallet, pulled out the card of the police detective, and punched in her number. She answered on the first ring, and I quickly identified myself. "Levi Rawdon is at Kachess Lake," I said. "He's hiking on one of the trails. He loves the mountains; that's where he's most at home — it's a spiritual thing for him. I'm sure he's there, or almost sure."

"Okay, Jonas," she said, her voice business-like. "That sounds plausible. I'll call the ranger station up there. I'll get back to you if I hear anything."

"Detective Brockman, he was just wearing sweats. If he's out on a trail — "

"If your friend is out on a trail, they'll put together a search team to find him. But you're way ahead of yourself, young man. You've got *ifs* piled on *ifs* piled on *ifs*. Wait for some facts."

After I hung up, I went downstairs. My dad was working at the Blue Jay, but I told my mother about the trail up at Kachess Lake. "You might just be right," she said. I caught her looking outside. The rain had started again, and rain in Seattle meant snow in the mountains.

"It rained last night too," I said. "And it was cold."

"There's a wool blanket in the trunk of the Subaru, and also one of your dad's sweatshirts. Remember, Levi knows the mountains. He knows how to take care of himself."

Back upstairs I checked my e-mail—there was one from Coach Richter with the subject heading: *Congratulations!* I didn't even open it. Around eleven I switched the light off, lay back on my bed, and closed my eyes. I kept my cell phone on the table next to me in case anyone called.

The next thing I knew, my dad was shaking me. "Jonas, wake up. They found Levi."

I sat up, completely alert. "At Kachess Lake? Was he there? Was I right?"

"He was there," he said, his voice strangely choked and thick.

"I knew he would be there. I was really starting to worry. That's great."

"No, no, Jonas. No. You don't understand."

"You said they found him."

My father put his arm around my shoulder, and I could feel him shaking. "They found his body. Levi is dead, Jonas. Your friend is dead."

13

I WENT DOWNSTAIRS, SAT ON THE SOFA, and drank a cup of tea that my mother made for me. I don't really like the taste of tea, but that night it didn't taste at all — it was just hot, and the heat felt good going down. When I finished the tea, I stepped outside the house and walked out into the street. Down the block, the lights in Levi's house were on, and two police cars were parked in front. I wanted to go to his house and hear what was being said, but I wasn't part of his family. I shuffled into my own home and was about to head up to my bedroom when a car pulled into our driveway. Within a minute there was a firm rap on the door.

It was Detective Brockman. "I don't have much time," she said, and then she told us what she knew. The Subaru had been where I'd thought it would be. Levi had gone up on the same trail we'd hiked in the summer. He was wearing a sweatshirt and sweatpants — no jacket, no sweater, and the temperature had dropped into the teens. "He wandered off the trail. Over a foot of snow fell Saturday night. Had he made himself some sort of shelter, he might have lived, but wearing what he was wearing . . . out in the open . . . he had no chance. The medical examiner will do a blood test to see if alcohol or drugs played a part, but it'll be a few weeks before the results are back." She paused. "I'm very sorry. What a terrible, terrible tragedy."

I didn't go to school Monday morning, but somehow my mom found out that there would be an assembly at eleven, and once I heard that, I had to be there. I arrived at Harding just as it started. Word of Levi's death must have gotten out, because kids were quiet as they headed into the gym, and they looked away when they saw me. I wanted to find somebody on the team, but it wasn't until I was inside the gym that I spotted Cash. "Do you think he was drunk like people are saying?" Cash whispered.

"No. Not Levi. You know that."

Cash look confused. "How do you explain it, then?"

Before I had to answer, Mr. Diaz's voice came over the speakers. "Students, please take a seat. This is not a time for fooling around. Just take the nearest open spot so we can begin. I have important information to give you."

The gym quieted, and then Mr. Diaz — in short, simple sentences — told the school of Levi's death. When he finished speaking, girls leaned on one another's shoulders and sobbed. Guys cradled their heads in their hands. Everybody at Harding High knew Levi — he was the six-six guy in the hallways who was kind to everybody.

Always.

I bowed my head and felt my shoulders shake. I couldn't let myself cry though, because if I started, I'd never stop.

Mr. Diaz saved me. After he'd let his words sink in, he said that counselors would be available for those who needed them. "You can stay here if you want, or you can go to your class, but I can't allow you to congregate in the hallways or in any of the other public areas. I'd ask you not to leave the school grounds, either."

Cash climbed down out of the bleachers and left without turning back. I wanted to get away too, but I couldn't make myself stand.

It was right then—right when my throat ached so much it was hard to breathe—that I saw Hartwell. He was speaking with Mr. Diaz, his face solemn, his eyes cast downward. I hated him; I hated him to the core. He killed my friend; he killed the best person I'd ever known, the best person I ever will know. He'd taken Levi's simple heart and twisted it until it had snapped.

Another teacher called to Mr. Diaz, and he moved toward her. Hartwell turned back toward the seats, and his eyes caught mine. He nodded—a nod of sorrow and sympathy. He took a step toward me and then another step.

I wanted to run, but I didn't. Instead, I came down out of the stands and walked toward him, walked fast and with a purpose. When I reached him, I could see distrust in his eyes. "I'm so—" he started.

"I know everything," I said, interrupting. "Levi told me. You're the reason he's dead."

Hartwell's eyes narrowed. "What are you talking about?"

"I'm talking about the snow camping. I'm talking about the times Levi went to your apartment for tutoring. He told me what happened."

Hartwell's back straightened, and his voice turned business-like. "Jonas, you're upset, and I understand that, but what you're saying makes no sense. Nothing happened on the camping trip. Nothing happened at my apartment."

"You're a liar, and I'm going to tell everyone. You're going to prison."

"Stop," he commanded. "Stop right there and come with me."

14

I DON'T UNDERSTAND WHY I FOLLOWED him to his office — maybe because he was a teacher and I was a student — but I followed him. He had me sit in a blue plastic chair while he sat in the swivel chair behind his desk.

"Let's be clear with one another. You're suggesting I abused Levi, right? That's what you're accusing me of." His voice was eerily calm, as if he were discussing the scouting report on an upcoming opponent.

"That's right," I answered, determined not to back down.

"And what is your proof?"

"He told me."

Hartwell smiled contemptuously. "He told you? We're talking about Levi, remember? Levi wouldn't even say the word *damn*. So what exactly did he tell you? That I did something bad? And that means what? That I drank a beer while I was tutoring him? It means nothing, Jonas. Nothing. And Mr. Diaz will send you right out the door."

As Hartwell's confident sentences filled the room, what had been clear became cloudy. I tried to remember the words Levi had used. Because Hartwell was right—Mr. Diaz, the police—they would want to know Levi's exact words. Had Levi ever used the word *sex*? Or was I the one who had said that word? Had I figured everything out from Levi's silences?

As Hartwell waited, I could feel his tension. When I said nothing, he exhaled loudly, and a look of triumph came to his face. "Here's why I know Levi didn't tell you anything—because there's nothing to tell. Levi and I went camping on New Year's Eve. Camping, that's all. I tutored him at my apartment. Tutoring, that's all. If he implied that I did anything wrong, then it was entirely in his imagination, or maybe in yours."

"Levi didn't imagine things," I said, my voice shaky, "and neither did I. You did things—I know you did. You can deny it all you want, but I'll never believe you."

Hartwell tapped the top of his desk with his fingertips, and then he folded his hands in front of his face, scorn in his eyes. "Don't believe me, then. That's your choice. But keep your sick thoughts to yourself, because if you accuse me of anything, if you try to take away my name and my career, then I'll fight you with everything I've got, and I'll win." He paused, and a little smile came to his lips. "You're sort of in a glass house, aren't you? You're not exactly in a position to throw stones. Or hadn't you thought about that?"

"What are you talking about?" I asked, baffled. "What glass house?"

"I'm talking about chemistry, Jonas. I'm talking about your scholarship to Monitor College. I was there right before you downloaded Butler's files and e-mailed them to yourself, remember?

I know the date, the computer, everything. If I were to tell the school district's tech guys, they'd have your e-mail tracked in ten minutes."

"My chemistry class has nothing to do with Levi."

"It has everything to do with you, though. If you go to Mr. Diaz with some crazy story that you *can't* prove, then you'll force me to tell him a real story that I *can* prove. Your B in chemistry will become an F, and your scholarship to Monitor College will evaporate. You'll brand yourself as a cheater, and you'll wear that label for the rest of your life. That's what you'll do to yourself. And what you'll do to Levi is even worse. Right now he's a hero. You start telling sex stories about him, and that's gone. Levi's father — you know what he's like. He'd hate the memory of his only son. Would you really do that to him, Jonas? And for what? This is America. A person is innocent until they're proven guilty, and you have no proof against me because nothing happened."

Hartwell let me sit for a while before he spoke again. "I've got a class to teach. Stay here and think this over. You'll see my way is best for everyone — you, me, and Levi."

He left, and I sat in that stupid plastic chair, staring at the basketball team photo on the wall behind Hartwell's desk. In the photo, Levi was standing next to me in the center. On one side was Mr. Knecht; on the other was Hartwell. Cash, Nick, De-Shawn, Brindle — they were mixed in with the other guys, all of us shoulder to shoulder, all of us smiling.

15

THERE WAS A MEMORIAL SERVICE in the school cafeteria the next night. Flowers covered tables up front, and on the walls were pictures of Levi. In every corner was a table with butcher paper and markers where kids could write whatever messages they wanted.

Levi's father spoke next, Levi's mother at his side. He said that God had a plan for all of us and that sometimes that plan was a mystery, and this is where faith came in. He stepped aside then, and others came to the podium to describe what Levi had meant to them.

Rachel spoke next. She described how much Levi had loved the mountains and how it was fitting that his life would end there. "My brother's soul is with God now," she said, and as she left the podium, her father hugged her. It was the first time I'd ever seen him hug any of his children.

After Rachel, a stream of students took the microphone to describe things Levi had done or said. Some of them were kids who never spoke in class and barely said a word in the halls. Invisible kids — not athletes, not great students, not anything. But they knew Levi. They weren't invisible to him.

Toward the end, I went up and said something about him being my friend, and how the word *friend* was the only word I could think of, but that it wasn't a big-enough word. Hartwell spoke last, describing what a great teammate Levi had been, but how he was even a greater person. If I could have blocked out his words, I would have.

My parents also came to the memorial. On the drive back to Tangletown, they discussed how moving the service had been. I agreed, but upstairs in my room with the door closed, I felt sick.

Everything people said had been true, but it hadn't been the whole truth. Nobody had said anything about Levi being called Dumb-Dumb or about how he was a kid who others teased — but that was also part of who he was, who he had been. He was getting whittled down, somehow. Death was doing that to him.

At school the next day, the hallways were hushed in the morning, but during each passing period, the volume grew. By lunchtime kids were laughing and talking loudly. And the next day, the hallways weren't quiet at all — not in the morning, not in the afternoon. Midterms were coming up, and after that came spring break and pretty soon graduation. People hadn't forgotten about Levi, but they were beginning to forget. All that time, I kept going over everything that had happened. All that time, I asked myself the same question: *What should I have done differently?*

I received a letter from Coach Richter giving details about orientation at Monitor College in late August. For two days, only freshman would be on campus. I'd get a feel for the school, see the athletic facilities, and meet some of my teammates. Richter wrote that there was no designated athletic dorm, but most of the guys lived at Hawthorne Hall, and he recommended I sign up for that. It was obvious he hadn't heard about Levi's death. Why would he? New Hampshire was three thousand miles away.

I showed Richter's letter to my mother, and she told me that I shouldn't feel guilty about moving on. "Levi would want you to go to Monitor College and do well. You know he would."

Friday before chemistry class, Celia told me that her volleyball coach had passed out free tickets to see the UW Husky women's basketball team play. "If you want, we could go together." I knew that it was a charity date, but I agreed.

My parents were happy when I told them why I wanted the car for Saturday night. "You need to get your own life going again," my dad said.

I sat next to Celia during the basketball game, but she spent most of the time talking to Cassie Holt, a girl I sort of knew from English class. Every so often my mind would drift and I'd think about Levi. I'd come out of it, talk about the game with Celia for a little bit, and then my mind would drift again. When the games ended, a handful of us went to Miro on Ballard Avenue, where we drank Italian sodas and listened to two guys playing Spanish guitars.

I took Celia home a little after midnight. "That was fun," she said, after I'd walked her to her front door. Instead of going inside, she stood looking at me. Maybe she was waiting for me to kiss her, I'm not sure. The moment passed. Then she had her key in the door, and after that I was walking back to my car.

I got up late Sunday morning. When I went downstairs, my dad shoved the sports page of the *Seattle Times* at me. "Look at page four," he said, before he headed out the door for work.

I took the newspaper to the kitchen table, put a couple of slices of bread in the toaster, and then glanced at the page. The headline jumped out at me:

RYAN HARTWELL NAMED HOOPS COACH OF THE YEAR

The article described Knecht's accident and the title run, and at the end it briefly mentioned Levi's death. My mom came into the kitchen as I finished reading. "Your father showed me," she said, nodding toward the newspaper. "I'm glad for Coach Hartwell. He deserved it. A young man facing all that's happened. He's handled it really well."

16

BEFORE SCHOOL ON MONDAY, A bunch of kids surrounded Hartwell, congratulating him on his award. He'd high-five one person, then bump knuckles with the next, while all the time the crowd grew larger. I slipped away before anyone could see me.

During lunch I didn't want to run into any of the guys on the team, so I ate outside on the steps by the parking lot. In six months I'd be three thousand miles from Seattle, taking classes at Monitor College, and all this would be in the past.

When the wind came up and rain started to fall, I headed back into the building, figuring the library would be a good place to kill the ten minutes before my next class.

I pushed through the turnstile and looked for an empty area. I walked past the fiction shelves to the rear wall and turned a corner. All alone at a small table sat Brandon, the sophomore on the team who'd almost never played. He gave me a wave and a smile, and I smiled back. I'd always liked Brandon — maybe because he reminded me of Levi. They were both on the shy side, and neither one of them ever had a mean word for anyone.

I was about to sit down across from him when I heard footsteps behind me. I turned and found myself face-to-face with Ryan Hartwell. I looked at him and then looked to Brandon, and the world seemed to shrink to that one small spot.

"Is he tutoring you?" I asked Brandon.

Brandon nodded, his face down. "Yeah, in geometry. I suck at math."

I turned back to Hartwell. Our eyes locked exactly as they had after Hartwell had knocked Knecht to the ground. Something had passed between us then. I knew what it was — I'd always known — but until that moment, I'd never admitted it to myself. That had been no accident, any more than Levi's death had been an accident. Hartwell had seen Knecht step onto the basketball court, and he had smashed him to the ground. He'd knocked the old man down so that he could take over the team. Hartwell did whatever he wanted. My eyes returned to Brandon. He was gazing at both of us, his face open and trusting just like Levi's had been.

Hartwell must have read my mind. "Don't do anything stupid, Jonas." His voice was soft but menacing. He was blocking my way, but I pushed by him. He followed as I moved toward the front desk of the library. "I'm warning you — don't play the hero. All you'll do is blow up your future."

"Maybe that's what I need to do," I said, spinning around to face him. "Maybe I need to blow everything up so I can start clean."

I turned back and took a few more steps. I was about to pass through the turnstile and head out of the library into the main hall when I felt his hand grasp my shoulder. "I'm not asking you. I'm telling you."

His fingers were like claws digging into my skin. I put my hand over his and wrested myself free. He resisted at first, but in the end he let me go. He looked at me while I was breaking free, trying to read what I'd do. I held his eyes for a while, but then I had to look away. His will was stronger than mine, just as it had been stronger than Levi's.

I left the library and walked down the main hallway of the school. My body was trembling; my face was on fire. I'd gone about fifty feet when I saw a side hallway at the end of which was a door leading to the parking lot.

I hurried to the door, pushed it open, and stepped outside. I sucked in the fresh air, trying to get control of myself. First lunch had ended; second lunch was about to begin. Cars were pulling in and out of parking spots; kids were piling in and out. Everyone seemed to be headed somewhere. But what about me? Where was I headed?

I stood, staring at all those cars, and the answer came.

Nowhere.

I could go three million miles away, and it wouldn't matter. I had no chance in the classroom at Monitor College, no chance on Coach Richter's basketball team, no chance to be a man — not unless I stood up to Hartwell.

17

WAS STILL SHAKY WHEN I stepped back into the school, so shaky I'd half forgotten where the main office was located. Somehow I got there; somehow I opened the door and went inside. My world was in turmoil, but everything in the office was completely ordinary. The secretary, Mrs. Wiley, looked up and smiled. "Can I help you, Jonas?"

"I need to see the principal right away," I said.

She shook her head. "You'll have to wait. Your coach is with Mr. Diaz now." She looked up at the clock. "Why don't you come back after school? Class will start in just a couple of minutes. You don't want to be late."

"Hartwell is in there with Mr. Diaz?"

"Yes, Mr. Hartwell is in there. Now unless this is extremely important, I . . ."

Before she could finish, I rushed past her desk and threw open the principal's door. Hartwell turned. When he saw me, his face went gray. Mr. Diaz jumped to his feet and came around from behind his desk. "Jonas, you have no business coming in here. You need to leave immediately."

"Hear me out," I said, pulling the door closed behind me and holding the doorknob so that no one could go in or out. "Just hear me out." I ignored Hartwell and instead looked straight at Mr. Diaz. "The stuff he's telling you about me cheating in chemistry—that's true. But he's not telling you what he did to Levi. Ask him about the trip he took with Levi to Mount Rainier on New Year's Eve. Ask him about the party he had on Labor Day, about the tutoring sessions he had with Levi in his apartment. Ask him about Brandon Taylor."

When I'd first stepped through the door, Mr. Diaz's thick eyebrows had narrowed and his eyes had turned into angry dark slits. But as I spoke, the anger was replaced by confusion. He looked to Hartwell, and then he looked back to me. "Are you saying what I think you're saying?" he asked.

I motioned toward Hartwell. "He's the reason Levi is dead," I whispered, fighting back the tears that were suddenly choking my words. "He did terrible things. You've got to stop him, or he'll do them to somebody else."

Mr. Diaz turned to face Hartwell. For a moment Hartwell's face was frozen, but then his mouth formed a strange smile. "This is ridiculous." He pointed at me. "I catch you cheating, and you rush in here with some crazy story. You are completely out of line." Hartwell reached across Mr. Diaz's desk and picked up the telephone. "Mr. Diaz, with your permission, I'll call security."

While Hartwell had been speaking, Mr. Diaz had kept his eyes fixed on me. I could feel my shoulders shaking, but I fought to keep control. I was not going to break down in front of Hartwell.

"Put the phone down, Mr. Hartwell," Diaz said.

"Excuse me?" Hartwell said.

"I said to put the phone down. Then please step outside and wait in the staff room for me."

"You want me to step outside?"

"I want you to step outside."

"What about Jonas?"

"Jonas is staying here with me."

Hartwell's odd smile disappeared. "You're not taking him seriously? You can't be. The kid is both a cheater and a liar. How can you possibly — "

"Mr. Hartwell, I want you to leave my office now. We'll talk later."

Hartwell stood still for a long moment and then threw his hands up. "All right. All right. I'm gone." I moved aside so he could get to the door. He turned the doorknob, looked back, and pointed a finger at me. "Making up stuff isn't going to work. The truth will come out. The more lies you tell, the worse it will be for you."

18

TOLD MR. DIAZ EVERYTHING, beginning with meeting Hartwell at Green Lake and ending with Brandon in the library. The beer, the R-rated movies, Butler's chemistry files, the New Year's Eve camping trip, Levi's tutoring sessions at Hartwell's apartment—I talked for thirty minutes straight. The hardest part was describing that night at the Good Shepherd Center. But I went through that for Mr. Diaz, too, going slowly and repeating Levi's words as best as I could remember them. While I talked, Mr. Diaz took notes, his body perfectly still, his pen moving smoothly over a yellow notepad.

When I finished, he leaned forward in his chair. "You know it's a crime to make a false accusation, don't you?"

"I know."

"And you know this won't change your chemistry grade."

"I know. I'll get an F. I'll lose the scholarship."

"But you stand by everything you've said."

"Everything."

"Okay, then."

He turned away from me, picked up his telephone, and dialed. I could faintly hear the phone ring once. A tinny voice came through the receiver. "Seattle Police Department. How can I help you?"

Twenty minutes later I was in a small conference room outside the principal's office telling my story to Detective McDowell from the police department. McDowell, a rumpled red-haired man with a belly that hung over his belt, took notes in a small flip notebook like the ones cops always have in movies.

While I'd been talking with Mr. Diaz, I could see the shock of my words reflected in his eyes. But McDowell's watery blue eyes didn't register at all; you'd have thought I was reading the school lunch menu. His face stayed blank even when I repeated Levi's confession to me at the Good Shepherd Center.

"So that brings us to today. Correct?" McDowell said, when I'd finished telling him about Hartwell meeting Brandon in the library.

"Right. That was just an hour ago."

McDowell raised his arms above his head, stretched a little, stuck out his lower lip, and slowly flipped back through his notes, mumbling to himself as he read. Finally he stood up. "I'll be back in a little while. You sit tight, okay?"

Before I fully understood what was happening, he'd left, closing the door behind him. I felt deserted. Fortunately, the room had a small window that looked out to the office area. Through it, I saw McDowell talk briefly to Mr. Diaz. Then both of them moved to a part of the office I couldn't see. A few minutes after that, I saw DeShawn enter the office, and then Nick and Brandon. I expected to see Cash come through the main door as well, but if he did, I missed him.

There was another meeting room next to where I was waiting. I heard the door open and close, and then I heard voices. I tried to make out what they were saying, but the words were muffled. I knew what was happening, though. Detective McDowell was questioning them about Hartwell, about me, and about Levi. What could they say? They didn't know anything. To them, Hartwell was a hero. Levi had told me, but he hadn't told anyone else.

Ten minutes passed . . . twenty minutes . . . thirty. The door in the adjacent room opened and closed. There was nothing but silence for a few minutes, and then there was a new voice. An adult voice. Had McDowell moved on to Hartwell? I couldn't be sure, but I thought so. The muffled voices talked on and on.

A full hour passed before the room next door at last went silent. My head ached, and I felt sick to my stomach. I had to wait five more minutes before the door to the room where I'd been confined opened. Detective McDowell came in, pulled out a chair, sat down across from me, took out that flip notebook of his, and silently read through the pages. Then he closed the notebook and leaned back in the chair and spoke. "Cash isn't at school today, but I talked to Nick and DeShawn. And I talked to Brandon too. They say Hartwell is a great guy and a great coach. They say there was no party, no beer, no porno movies. Not on Labor Day or on any other day."

"Brandon didn't play at Green Lake in the summer," I said, frustrated. "He wasn't at the party. And the other guys are covering for Hartwell. I told you that he made us promise not to tell. It's got to be in your notes. And they weren't porno movies; they were R-rated. I told you that, too."

Instead of answering, McDowell tapped his fingers together, sizing me up as he did. Finally he spoke. "I talked to Coach Hartwell. He also insists there was no party, no beer, no movies, nothing improper on Mount Rainier or during any of his tutoring sessions. He says you're trying to get back at him because he caught you cheating."

"He helped me cheat," I said, trying not to get angry. "I explained that before. All of this has got to be in your notes. He led me to the teachers' workroom in the back of the library. How would I have even known about that computer without his help?"

Detective McDowell leaned toward me. "If you need to change your story, now is the time to do it. You take this too far, and you could find yourself in serious trouble."

"Every word I told you was the truth."

He rubbed his chin for a while, then stood, walked over to the door, and opened it. "You can leave now, Jonas. But I'll be talking to you again."

It was half a threat, half a promise.

19

I KNEW THAT SOONER OR LATER I'd have to tell my parents everything — but that night I didn't have the energy. My dad was at work, so it was just my mom and me at dinner. Even though I tried to be upbeat, she sensed something was wrong. Twice she asked if I felt all right, and twice I lied. I was glad to be able to escape to my room.

I opened my laptop, and for a few hours was clicking from one sports website to another. I even read articles on golf. When it was late enough, I flicked off the light and climbed into bed. I couldn't sleep, so I lay on my back and looked at the ceiling.

Cash was my last chance. I tried to convince myself that he'd back me up, but inside I didn't believe it. We'd meshed well on the court, but off the court we'd never even eaten lunch together. He was one of Hartwell's guys. They were all Hartwell's guys. Hartwell had taken us to the top of the mountain. They weren't going to throw him over a cliff, not for me.

I turned my light back on. On the table next to my bed was the color brochure from Monitor College. I picked it up and flipped through it. The ivy-covered brick buildings, the snowy winters, the basketball court, the classes — gone. All of it gone.

I flicked the light off and managed to sleep some, but when I awoke the next morning, my mouth was dry, my throat was sore, and my eyelids felt as if there were sandpaper underneath them. I took a shower, ate a piece of toast, and headed out the door. "Have a good day," my mom said as I left.

If ever I wanted a gray Seattle day, it was that morning. But instead of being cloudy, the sky overhead was an incredible baby blue. Big white clouds sat like cotton balls high in the sky, and a bright morning sun warmed my face. The universe seemed to be mocking me.

I looked over at Levi's house as I walked past, and I remembered all those summer afternoons when I'd been so eager to get moving, off to play basketball. I thought about Levi's sisters never again having Levi around to pick them up, twirl them about, and tell them they were princesses.

When I stepped inside Harding High that morning, I felt strangely out of place. I kept expecting to see Detective McDowell looking for me in the hallway or to hear my name called over the intercom system, but nothing happened.

I made it through English and algebra, though I'm not sure how. After those classes, it was time for chemistry with Butler. I didn't know what I should do. Had he been told about me? It had seemed like a year, but it had been only one day. Who would have told him?

I milled around outside his door until just before the bell rang. Then, because Celia was the last friend I had, I slipped inside Butler's classroom. It was a huge mistake. When he spotted me,

Butler pointed his pudgy finger at me. "You. You have the nerve to come in here? Step out into the hall and wait for me there."

I felt dizzy, but I did what he said. As I stood outside his door, he growled something to the class, and then he was in my face. "Needless to say, you have an F for last semester and for this one too. Also, you are not in my class anymore. Is what I'm saying clear?"

I nodded. "It's clear. I just wanted to say that —"

"I don't want to hear anything that you have to say. Save your phony apologies for somebody else." He strode back into the classroom, pulling the door closed with a bang and leaving me alone in the empty hallway.

I looked around. Where was I supposed to go? I couldn't stand around for an hour, not without catching the notice of somebody. The only safe place I could think of was the library, so that's where I went.

I found an empty table in the back and tried to read a book about airplanes that was lying on the table, but that was hopeless. I dreaded the rest of the day: American government, lunch, Spanish, health. And if I got through today, what next? Another day, and another, and another — all the way until June. Beads of sweat formed on my forehead. How could I survive all those days?

I felt like a trapped animal, so I looked around for a way out. The main library door led back into the school, but a side door to my left opened out to the parking lot. A sudden thought came to me. What was to stop me from walking out that very minute and never returning? I had no real friends at Harding High. Nobody would miss me. I could take a couple of classes online or at a community college and get my diploma that way. I didn't need Harding High.

Right then a girl who'd played on Celia's volleyball team entered the library. She glanced around, spotted me, smiled, and started walking toward me. She was a junior, but she looked more like a seventh-grader — round face, freckles, eyes that were a little too wide open. I couldn't remember her name, but I knew she was an office TA because I'd seen her the day before. "You're Jonas Dolan, aren't you?" she asked when she reached my table.

"Yeah, I'm Jonas."

She laughed nervously. "I don't know why I asked. I know who you are. Everybody knows who you are. I went to all the basketball games. Well, not all of them, but the ones at the end. You played great. It was so exciting."

"Thanks."

She stood still for an instant, and then she shoved a blue piece of paper toward me. "This is for you. When I didn't find you in your chemistry class, I thought you might be here, and I guessed right."

I took the pass from her, opened it, and read it. Her voice became serious. "That policeman is with Mr. Diaz again — the one who was here yesterday. He had Cash with him all of second period. You guys aren't in trouble, are you?"

"No, we're not in trouble."

She smiled again. "Good." She paused. "I think they want you there right now."

I took a deep breath and then walked to the main office. I handed my pass to Mrs. Wiley, and within minutes I was back in the small conference room telling Detective McDowell the same exact things I'd told him the day before. As I spoke, he flipped through his notebook, checking my new words against my old ones. I could sense his irritation from the angry way he turned the small pages.

"I spoke with Cash this morning," he said when I finished. "Do you know what he told me? That there was no party on Labor Day. Or beer. Or raunchy movies. He said there was no hint of anything inappropriate in Coach Hartwell's behavior at any time during the entire season."

"He's lying."

"So what you're saying about Coach Hartwell has nothing to do with the fact that he caught you cheating?"

"No. Nothing."

"Nothing to do with the fact that because of him you're going to lose your basketball scholarship?"

"No."

"Hartwell turns you in for cheating, and then five minutes later you just happen to walk into Mr. Diaz's office with your accusations. It's all a big coincidence."

"I've explained everything. Over and over, I've explained it."

McDowell put his fingertips on his forehead and closed his eyes for a few seconds. He sighed and then opened them. "So we're right back where we were yesterday. You, Jonas Dolan, are telling the truth. Everyone else is lying."

I didn't bother to answer.

McDowell stared at me for a long time. Then, abruptly, he stood. "Come with me," he said, and he was out the door so fast that I had to hurry to keep up.

I followed him to the conference room where he had spoken

with me the day before. He opened the door and pointed. "In there." I slid past him and then stopped quickly. In front of me was Cash. He was slouched in one of those uncomfortable plastic chairs, his arms folded across his chest, a scowl on his face.

Cash did a double take when he saw me, and then we both looked to Detective McDowell for an explanation. McDowell's eyes were heated, and so was his voice. "I've got lots to do, gentlemen, and I have no more time for this nonsense. I tap-danced around yesterday with two contradictory stories, and I've tap-danced around today with two contradictory stories, but I'm not tap-dancing anymore. You two were the team captains. You pulled together and won a state championship. If you get along on the court, then by God you can do it off the court too. I'm going to leave you alone in here for ten minutes. When I come back into this room, I expect to hear one story. The true story."

Before either of us could object, McDowell was gone.

20

I LOOKED TO CASH. HIS HEAD was down, his eyes fixed on the carpet, his face blank. I waited. "Why are you doing this, Jonas?" he said at last.

"For Levi."

He looked up, his mouth twisted into a scowl. "For Levi? You've got to be kidding. Right now Levi is a legend, and he could stay a legend, if you don't ruin it for him and for us."

"I'm not the one who ruined it."

He put his head in his hands and stared at the floor again. "That cop — McDowell — he's asked me the same questions over and over. *Did Hartwell have us over to his apartment? Did Hartwell give us beer? Did Hartwell show us dirty movies?* You want me to rat him out and get him fired over a couple of beers and some movies? After all he's done for us?"

"Come on, Cash. It's not over a couple of beers and some movies, and you know it. It's more than that. McDowell must have told you."

"Yeah, yeah," Cash snapped, "I know. You say Hartwell's a pervert."

"Levi said it. He said it to me."

Cash frowned. "Hartwell called me last night. He says you're making up this stuff because he caught you cheating in chemistry. He says you're trying to get back at him."

"It's true that I cheated. But the rest of what he said is a lie."

"So I'm supposed to believe you and not him? That's what it comes to, right?"

"I guess. But do you really think Levi got lost that night? Or that he was drunk or on drugs? Because I don't."

"I don't either," Cash admitted after a long pause. "Not Levi." Then he leaned toward me and spoke, almost a whisper. "But don't you see, Jonas. If it comes out that Hartwell is a pervert, and that we were at his house drinking with him and watching sexy movies with him — you know what everybody is going to think? They're going to think he was doing stuff with us, too."

"They won't think that," I said.

His nostrils flared. "Yeah, they will. You know they will. And if you don't know it, then you're a fool."

He stopped, and the room went quiet. I looked at the clock; McDowell would soon be coming through the door again.

"Did you hear I got a basketball scholarship to Western?" Cash said, the anger gone from his voice.

"No. I didn't. When did that happen?"

"A couple of days ago. That's why I wasn't at school yesterday. I drove up to Bellingham to meet the head coach and sign the papers. He had somebody else lined up, but that guy switched to a different school. The Western coach was at the Tacoma Dome and saw us beat Garfield. He says he likes my game, likes the fact that I was a team player."

"That's great, Cash. That's fantastic."

Cash stretched his legs out in front of him and then sat up straight. "I was never a team player until you came along."

His words — his praise — took me by surprise. I didn't know how to answer, but I didn't have to reply because the door opened and Detective McDowell stepped inside. Our ten minutes were up. McDowell looked at me and then looked at Cash. "So which one of you is going to tell me what happened?"

Neither of us spoke. Seconds ticked away. Each second seemed like a minute; each minute felt like an hour.

"Do you need more time?" McDowell said at last. "Because I can go outside and wait for another ten minutes, and for another ten minutes after that. I'll wait all day if I have to, but I will get one answer."

More silence. "Okay. See you in ten minutes."

He opened the door and was about to leave when Cash spoke. "There wasn't *one* party," he said.

I felt the blood rush out of my face; a roaring started in my ears. I looked into Cash's face. I was expecting to see ice, but instead he sort of nodded to me, a nod of reassurance, and then he turned away so that he was facing Detective McDowell. "There were at least four parties, and maybe more that I don't know about. Levi and Jonas weren't invited after they walked out of the first one, but Coach Hartwell kept asking the rest of us to his apartment. Each time he had more beer for us; each time the movies got raunchier. The last time — this would have been about a month ago — he said we could stay overnight, but nobody did."

McDowell sat down, took out his small notebook, and calmly wrote for a few minutes. When he finished, he looked at Cash. "So why didn't you tell me this earlier?"

Cash shrugged. "I promised Coach Hartwell I wouldn't tell. I gave him my word of honor. We all did. And . . ." His voice trailed off.

McDowell tilted his head. "And what?"

"And I like Coach Hartwell. Or at least I used to. We all liked him." Cash turned his eyes to me. "You liked him too, right?"

I nodded. "Yeah, I liked him." I turned to face McDowell. "He was the coach I wanted."

21

ONCE CASH TOLD THE TRUTH, Nick and DeShawn stopped lying too. In a TV show, McDowell would have arrested Hartwell, there'd have been a trial, and then a jury would have sent him to prison for fifty years.

But life isn't a TV show.

Instead of arresting Hartwell, for the next few days McDowell repeatedly called me out of class and into the conference room, where he questioned me, checking and rechecking everything to get it exactly right. Finally, after three separate interviews, he flipped through his notebook and closed it up. "That's it, at least for now."

"You mean I'm done?"

"For now."

I started to leave but then sat back down. "There's going to be a trial, right? Hartwell won't get away with it, will he?"

McDowell sat frozen for a moment. I could feel him thinking. At last he leaned forward toward me. "The alcohol is where we're sure to get him. He provided it to minors repeatedly over months. I'm not going to lie to you, though. That's a class-one misdemeanor charge, which means it's serious, but it's not a felony.

Hartwell might go to jail for a year but no longer. The important thing is — the conviction will be on his record forever. He will never teach again. He will never coach again. And I promise you that I will do everything in my power to keep him from having anything to do with kids in any capacity. This man is on my radar, and he's on my radar forever."

"But Levi? What about the things he did to Levi? Won't there be a trial about that?"

McDowell slowly shook his head. "Probably not. As far as we know, Levi was his only victim. That's good, Jonas. Nobody wants victims. But . . ." McDowell stopped and looked at his hands.

"But Levi is dead," I said, calmly finishing his sentence for him. "Levi can't testify. It would be my word against Hartwell's, and that's no good in court. Hartwell told me that, and he was right."

McDowell sat straight up; his eyes honed in on mine and held them. "Listen to me, and listen good. Don't ever think that what you did was for nothing. You stood up to Hartwell, and you stopped him. Okay, maybe he isn't going to prison for what he did to Levi. But that doesn't change the fact that you saved people. You'll never see their faces or know their names, but you saved them. You're a hero, Jonas. Do you hear what I'm saying? A hero. Don't ever doubt it, and don't ever forget it."

22

WHEN I LEFT SCHOOL THAT day, I had one thing left to do, and that was to explain everything to my parents. They'd hate Hartwell, but what would they think of me?

As I was heading up the steps to my home, my dad was just opening the front door to leave for work. I wanted to get it over with, so I asked him to stay a few minutes. "I need to talk to you and Mom."

There must have been something in my face or my voice, because he didn't ask any questions. He simply stepped back inside the house and walked to the kitchen, with me a few steps behind. My mom looked at the two of us. "What is it?" she asked.

Telling the story didn't take long. My mom's eyes welled up when I described the night at the Good Shepherd Center; my dad's eyes got fiery. When I finished, my mom told me that it took courage to speak up and that she was proud of me. "You got yourself lost," my dad said. "The important thing is to find your way back. I know you can do it."

✤ ✤ ✤

That conversation happened three weeks ago. Since then, I've been up and down, as if I'm on a never-ending roller-coaster ride. Sometimes I believe the good things that Detective McDowell and my mom and dad said about me. Sometimes I think about Levi and Hartwell and what I could have done differently, and I feel more lost than ever.

Which brings me to today. For weeks the sky has been gray, but this morning came up warm and sunny. After all the gloomy winter months of Seattle, it is as if the houses and trees are inching out of the shadows and into the light.

As usual, I walked to school, passing Levi's house along the way. Bikes and toys are still strewn around the front lawn. It seems somehow impossible that the house should look the same, but it does.

When I reached Harding, I went to my locker, talked tennis with Gokul, and then made it through my first two morning classes. I saw Celia during the passing period between second and third period. She waved and half smiled, and I waved back, which is what we always do now when we see each other.

I shelved books in the library during the hour when I should have been in chemistry. Then I went to my American government class, where Mrs. Clements led a discussion about the link between unemployment and crime.

When government class ended, I took a sack lunch onto the back steps and ate alone with the warm sunlight on my face. I was about half done when Rachel came out and sat down next to me. She was wearing a skintight, low-cut top again, so things are closer to normal for her.

We talked about the warm weather for a little bit, and then we just sat, both of us remembering Levi. "What are you going to do once you graduate?" she asked. "Are you still going to that college back East?"

"No, that's off. I'm not sure what I'm going to do. How about you? Have you got plans?"

"You bet I do. I've got lots of plans. I'm going to get my driver's license, and then I'm going to get a job so I have my own money. I'm also going to help my mom around the house and do more with my sisters. They miss Levi a lot." The whole time she spoke, her voice was strong and decisive.

The warning bell for fifth period rang. We both stood; Rachel smiled. "You should make a plan, too, Jonas. Figure out what's right for you, and then go out and do it." It felt strange to get a pep talk from Rachel, but before I could answer, she hugged me and then hurried off, leaving me alone.

The afternoon classes were the same as usual. I came home around three o'clock to an empty house, ate some peanut butter with crackers in the kitchen, and then went to the den.

I turned the television to ESPN. On the screen, a huge guy was lifting up the end of a telephone pole. I glanced away, and that's when I noticed my basketball over in the corner of my room. Seeing it gave me an uneasy feeling, so I looked back to the muscleman, who was now dragging the telephone pole down a gravel path, his checks puffing. It was too stupid to watch. I flicked off the television, picked up my basketball, and headed over to the Good Shepherd Center.

I'd been away from the game for so long that the ball actually felt strange in my hands. I didn't get a good release on my first couple of shots, didn't have any lift with my first tentative jumps.

And when I finally made a few baskets, I didn't feel the tingle of pleasure that I'd always felt when a basketball tickles the twine.

That's when I got angry.

Because I couldn't let Hartwell take basketball from me too.

I started moving more freely, shooting more freely, and pretty soon I was playing games in my head, taking down the Duke Blue Devils for the national title, leading a fast break against the Lakers — fantasy stuff that I've done for as long as I can remember. It was stupid, but the more I did it, the more like *me* I felt.

I swished a long three-pointer, a beautiful high-arcing shot. As I chased the down ball, I remembered what Rachel had said. Suddenly I knew what was right for me.

I grabbed the basketball, hurried home, looked up Mr. Knecht's number, and telephoned him. "Sure, I can help you," he said, after I explained what I wanted. "Shoreline Community College is the place you want to be, all right. I know the basketball coach there. I'll give him a call and put in a plug for you. Shoreline is a good school too. I mean academically. It'll prepare you for a four-year college."

I thanked Mr. Knecht and then went upstairs to my computer and downloaded the application form. It's sitting on the desk in front of me right now. I'll fill it out in a couple of minutes and take it to the post office tonight.

That's step one, and there are going to be a whole bunch of steps to follow.

Hartwell is not going to steal my life from me. I'm going to work hard both on the basketball court and in the classroom. And when my two years at Shoreline are done, I'm going to scratch my way into some college somewhere. I'm going to play basketball for that college, and I'm going to graduate from that college, and when I graduate, my dad is going to buy me that beer.

The sunlight that lit up the world this morning? I'm going to make it back into that sunlight. I'm going to do all these things for myself, and I'm going to do them for Levi, too.

I owe him.

DO YOU NEED HELP?

Speak with a trusted parent, teacher, counselor, or religious leader. If you need help immediately, call 911. Your safety matters.

LOOKING FOR MORE INFORMATION?

Visit these websites for information about ways to end sexual violence and build healthy lives:

- www.stopitnow.org
- www.rainn.org